STANDPIPES AND STORM SHELTERS

The Story of
Butterflies and Miracles
Continues

A NOVEL

by SANDI MCREYNOLDS

ISBN-13: 978-0692702727 (VineTree Press)

ISBN-10: 0692702725

 VineTree Press

FOR

Joplin Tornado Victims who still search for "normal."

Disaster Victors, wherever they are, who refuse to be defeated.

Kim, who shows the world how to face her fears and still find God faithful.

And Mac, who still encourages me.

In *Stand Pipes and Storm Shelters*, McReynolds truly finds her voice—a voice that needs to be heard. She deftly and accurately weaves a tale of adversity, hopelessness, and ultimate redemption. The readers quickly feel with the Morris family as they struggle with the devastating aftermath of tragedy, but also experience real encounters with hope and faith. An equally entertaining and touching read, *Stand Pipes* will empress you with the amazing impact of believers in a true community of faith.

Dr. Karl Wendt
Director, Mt. Hope Christian Counseling Center

CONTENTS

AUTHOR'S NOTE

It is said that every writer must sooner or later write a "book of the heart." *Butterflies at the Window,* a novel based on true stories of the 2011 Joplin Tornado, was mine. Manifold accounts of tragedy and triumph and miracles and butterfly people were so personal, so awe-inspiring and painful, they had to be written.

Much of what the McConnell family experienced in that book originated with our own family and friends. Like the entire Joplin area, our lives were forever changed by that monstrous storm. As temporary housing was erected north of town for the thousands of families whose homes were swept away, it soon became impossible to drive by those acres of institutional-looking boxes without reliving a little of that unspeakable time again. Even though the McConnell's journey had ended in hope and optimism, the unrelenting reality was that far too many were still adrift there, still longing for a better day, and their saga of God's mercy and love had only begun.

I first encountered Jax Morris as the McConnell's story was unfolding. Then, he was merely an unnamed tornado victim who furiously rejected their attempt to reach out to his family. Though he warranted only brief mention in that account, somehow the specter of such a sad, angry man haunted me; so when real-life disaster assistance sent me into that sprawling FEMA settlement, he seemed to follow me along those despair-ridden streets.

Eventually, as survivors who lived there began finding jobs and relocating to permanent homes, their vacated trailers were picked up and hauled away like so many discarded containers, leaving only disconnected electrical standpipes and ugly concrete storm shelters to stand guard over empty, desolate lots. The diminishing need for refuge was welcome confirmation of the community's growing recovery; but as temporary homes vanished one by one, a faint melancholy lingered. And it seemed to echo the pain of a desperate man who would not let me rest.

A little over two years after the tornado, only a few bleak units still remained, scattered here and there among those abandoned standpipes and storm shelters. Watching that long-drawn-out metamorphosis, one could not help but wonder how anyone still consigned to such a forlorn environment must be feeling. It was then that Jaxon James Morris II finally came knocking at my door; and God's amazing story of redemption—and butterflies in the storm—continued.

PROLOGUE

Jax Morris was already struggling with overwhelming anger, overwhelmed with fear for his family's future. Then the McConnell's showed up at the door of the dismal little FEMA dwelling that was now their home.

It had been six months since the tornado and his shattered leg still was not healing. He could tolerate being upright only a minute or two before pain defeated him again. He'd just struggled out of his wheelchair on that Thanksgiving morning, determined to stay up a little longer this time, when the knock had come. He was not a cruel man, but the sight of a happy, intact family offering charity to his, knowing he could no longer support and protect them, was the final blow to his fragile self-respect. His last reserve had shattered. He'd stood speechless, oblivious to his pain, as the blood had rushed to his head. Suddenly fear and anger had coalesced into consuming rage; and he'd slammed the door in their faces.

He'd been convinced that a move to someplace completely different, where nothing would remind him of the past, was what they'd needed. They'd been through too much heartbreak in too short a time and he could not stay where it all had happened. Only weeks after a fiery crash on an icy Michigan road had killed his wife's parents, an out-of-nowhere brain tumor had claimed his own mother. Then, one evening shortly after she'd died, Pops had gone home from after-work drinks with the guys, stretched out in his recliner, and died, too. Jax had never realized how much he'd depended on big, boisterous J. J. Morris for everything from opinions about life to advice about work until suddenly he was gone. He'd been desperate to get away from the pain.

For a while it had seemed to be working. Life had slowly become meaningful and pleasant again. They were actually beginning to feel at home in their new community. Then suddenly, on a perfect Sunday in May, their world had been turned upside down and inside out. Now he was terrified their family might not survive the damage that had been done. Now he was just marking time in this dreary trailer, hoping against hope that he would someday walk again... that he could find some way to work again... that his family might somehow become whole again...

STANDPIPES and STORM SHELTERS
April, 2013

Jax stood in the open door, leaning on the cane he despised, grimly surveying his surroundings. Nothing left as far as he could see, he thought bitterly, except those blasted abandoned standpipes and ugly useless storm shelters.

He'd hated those unsightly concrete boxes since he'd first seen them two years ago. They were a painful, in-your-face reminder that Jax Morris was as vulnerable as any man. He still shuddered to think of the terrifying night that had taught him that lesson. In less than a heartbeat a monstrous storm had turned their pleasant, ordered world into chaos and he hadn't even been able to protect himself, let alone the people he loved most. For the first time in his life, he'd been helpless and afraid.

Jaxon James Morris II was a man's man, even more rugged and burly than the father he'd idolized. Like his father, he was proud of his blue-collar heritage. The skills J. J. Morris had taught him as a teen-ager in Michigan had always been his strength and identity and he'd loved to boast that he was just like his father. They both could work and fight and drink any man under the table, he often declared to any who would listen. Unlike his father, however, he'd found his greatest meaning in his family. He loved them fiercely.

He'd adored beautiful, dark-haired Marianna Guarino since grade school. As a young bride, she'd been patient with his need to unwind with the guys after work, but when Jaxon James III was born, followed by Edward Roy two years later, evenings at the bar with the guys had eagerly become evenings at home with his guys.

Shortly after the sudden death of his father he'd moved his young family to Southwest Missouri where he hoped he'd find relief from the lingering ache in his heart. It had been a good move. There, his plumbing business had flourished. There, Marianna had cheerfully set about making their new house a home and the boys had found new friends. And there, Angelina Marianna had graced their lives. His little Angel was a blue-eyed, blond-haired throwback to the Morris clan's Scots heritage and Jax had found himself more madly in love than he'd ever thought possible. Surely no man had ever been so favored by whatever gods decided such things.

All that had changed on May 22, 2011. The EF5 tornado that struck their adopted town would quickly be labeled "the storm of the century." It had taken only twenty minutes for the mile-wide monster to roar through the city, but it had left the Morris's and thousands of other families devastated and homeless. Now his children struggled with the night, still haunted by the terror of that dark time. Now their father struggled with the day, still facing months of therapy on his shattered leg, still hoping it would eventually support him without this blasted cane, still fearful he might never work again. Now, they no longer enjoyed the friendly, middle-class neighborhood where their newly-remodeled home had anchored their lives. Since that fateful night, they'd simply survived in the sweeping "FEMA Village" that had sprung up northwest of the city.

As soon as FEMA had secured the site across from the old municipal airport, the agency had built those huge, unappealing concrete shelters; positioning them strategically throughout the project and around the outer perimeter; adding temporary housing units as tornado survivors were approved for them. Most of the displaced families living there were truly grateful. Having a home—even a featureless, temporary one—made rebuilding shattered lives seem somehow possible and the storm shelters helped restore a sense of security that had been cruelly blown away. Even so, one could hardly help but be depressed by such dreary surroundings. Not a tree or blade of grass remained in what had once been flourishing hay fields. Now those cheerless acres were crisscrossed by narrow streets lined by row after mind-numbing row of identical rectangles looking for all the world like drab little white mobile homes without wheels.

At least their unit was at the very back of the project, Jax had consoled himself. He'd rather look at trailers than those awful storm shelters. One by one, though, as families relocated to the homes and apartments that were being rebuilt, the uninviting rectangles had begun disappearing. Now, only a few scattered modules remained. This morning the trailer across the street had been moved out, leaving the Morris's isolated in a network of empty drives and deserted electrical standpipes. Word was that the storm shelters would eventually be sold to local organizations, but for now they dominated barren fields that had once been teeming with the wounded community in which they'd become unwilling participants.

He should call Marianna. He knew she was hurting as much as he was, though she seemed to have found some comfort in her new friends. He was not at all happy with the idea that his wife had become a church goer, but he had to admit he was a little surprised—even disappointed maybe?—that she'd never asked him to go with her.

He couldn't blame her for leaving, though. In fact, he'd been relieved when she'd taken the kids and moved to that Zimmerman place in Carthage. This rage that consumed him now terrified him even more than it had her, and at least there they had the peace and security he could no longer give them. What probably scared him even more, though, was that he seldom even missed them. If he dared allow any emotion at all into his big frame, he could risk only the anger that drove him.

His hand tightened on the head of his cane as a big white SUV turned off Highway 171 and headed his way. Ethan! His first impulse was to close the door and pretend he wasn't here. He had to admit at times it helped to feel like at least one person in this miserable world remembered he existed; but he still couldn't figure out why this man who seemed to have everything going for him was so determined to connect with him.

At first he'd thought it was some sort of "survivor guilt," like they'd talked about in those first sessions of disaster relief counseling. (He probably should have made sure his family stayed in that program longer, but it seemed like he'd come home from every session angrier than before they'd gone and Marianna had refused to go without him.)

Then he'd found out Ethan's family had been through even more than his, so he'd decided maybe the guy was one of those do-gooders who insisted on sticking their noses in other people's business. But if that was all it was, why would he keep coming back; even when Jax was downright rude at times? It seemed like no matter what he did, Ethan just wouldn't give up. Finally he'd had to admit he wanted that friendship. Whether he liked it or not, this man he couldn't begin to understand had become his only real ally in this strange new world.

His ruddy face colored a deep red as he remembered the first time he'd met the McConnell family. Those poor kids were so excited about bringing Thanksgiving baskets to people in the Village, but he'd been outright nasty and slammed the door in their faces. The idea of someone offering his family a handout had felt like the final blow to his manhood. He knew that didn't excuse bad manners, though. Ethan insisted he understood, but Jax still felt embarrassed about it. He'd have been furious if someone had treated his kids that way. But they'd just left the box at the door and quietly disappeared. Marianna had found a note Ethan had scribbled to him in the bottom of the box: "We'll be praying for your family this holiday season. Believe it or not, I really do understand what you're going through, and I know God has a plan in all this heartache. I'll try to catch you in a week or so. I think we have a lot to talk about."

"Yeah, right," he'd thought bitterly. "I can already see we have so much in common."

Actually, he'd been shocked that they did have a lot in common. Ethan's wife and kids had been trapped in the tornado, too, and he'd struggled with the same helpless panic that haunted Jax. According to Ethan, they'd worked through his dad's heart attack and his wife's paralysis; then the little ones' nightmares and his older daughter's guilt and grief before he'd realized the toll it was taking. He'd eventually broken, and their marriage had been falling apart when they'd finally gotten help from some trusted friends.

Why would a man like Ethan share all that with anyone? It did sound a lot like his story, but he still couldn't bring himself to risk trusting anyone, even Ethan McConnell. He was glad Marianna had been able to, though—glad she'd found something good in her life—but their so-called God would sure never bother with a guy like him. Especially when he'd spent his whole life denying he even existed.

"Hey Jax. Ready?"

He jumped at Ethan's greeting. He'd been so busy feeling sorry for himself he'd forgotten he was almost here. It wasn't that he didn't appreciate the help. He wasn't sure how he'd have made it to all his medical appointments after Marianna left if it hadn't been for Ethan, and he had to admit their late breakfast every Wednesday had pretty much become the bright spot of his week. He smiled in spite of himself, remembering Ethan's pronouncement: Jax was getting out of that house for some R & R if Ethan had to hogtie him. He'd laughed for the first time in months at that. "Hogtie" wasn't even a word where he came from.

5

Well, he was glad for the ride, even when he felt like he did today, so he needed to at least try to be grateful. Maybe today he'd even risk trying to trust a little. Or not.

2

PAINFUL BEGINNINGS

"We're seeing some warning signs in the boys, Jax," Ethan said quietly.

Jaxon felt a familiar flush of rage. Who did he think he was! J and Eddy Roy were his boys, not Ethan's. Then, as quickly as the anger had come, it was gone, leaving him drained. He looked down at his just-replenished coffee cup, big shoulders slumping in defeat. So much for good intentions. But if Ethan noticed, he hadn't reacted.

"Frank and I both thought they were adjusting pretty well until a couple weeks ago. They'd made new friends at church and there's no question they were excited about soccer, especially when they found out Frank and Ginny were planning to come to the games with their mom. But then, all of a sudden they just shut down—both of 'em. Marianna found Eddy Roy sobbing in the middle of the night and he wouldn't tell her why. When she asked J if he knew, he got furious and shouted they both wanted to quit soccer. He finally admitted to Frank... that man sure has a way with kids... that they didn't want to play anymore because all the other kids' fathers came to the games and theirs didn't. They're awesome kids and we all love 'em, Jax, but they're really needing their dad. We'll do whatever we can to help but no one can take your place."

Red-rimmed brown eyes came up at that. Ethan thought he'd never seen more pain in any human being; even during the worst of the tornado. Looking into those eyes was like taking a physical blow. He had no idea how to address such agony, so he waited as a range of emotions played across his friend's face.

"I-I'm so scared, Ethan." Jax was horrified. He couldn't believe he'd just said out loud what he hadn't even admitted to himself. Pops would never... But Pops was dead and the dam had broken and he couldn't seem to stop. His eyes fell again.

"I can't get on top of this rage. It just takes over and the only way I know to protect my family is to stay away. I can't even think about it. It kills me that I'm missing what my kids are doing. I'm petrified I'm losing my family and I can't do a thing about it. Marianna's the only woman I've ever loved—ever will—but she's not safe with me." Almost to himself he mumbled hoarsely, "What am I gonna do?"

The silence went on and on. Finally he looked up and his jaw dropped. Tears were streaming down Ethan's face. In public!

"Man, buddy! I know you won't believe this, but I've been exactly where you are, and not all that long ago. I couldn't get the ghosts of that night out of my head—most of all the people I couldn't help—and every time I saw my wife in that wheelchair, I felt like a failure. I should have been there to protect her and my kids. I still can't forget how I felt when I couldn't find Elly, or what I saw looking for her. No one should ever have to see things like that. Still don't know why I turned down 20th Street—well, there's really only one explanation—but when I finally found her and she told me her best friend was gone, I almost lost it right there. Then she insisted a huge man with wings had rescued Ali from that drainage ditch and taken her for help, and I thought *she'd* lost it. And when both the Littles kept insisting there were "butterfly guys" that protected them, part of me just shut down. For a long time I kinda stumbled through. Didn't even realize how it was all building up on me until Liz and I were so far apart we didn't even know how to find ourselves again, let alone each other."

"How did you..."

"A lot of prayer from a lot of friends, and tough love from some very special ones. We're both eternally grateful that God didn't give up on us. Frank and Ginny didn't either, and they had the courage to call us on what we were doing. Talk about 'speaking the truth in love.' We both knew we'd better turn it all over to the Lord or we wouldn't make it, but neither of us could seem to find Him. Still kinda scares me to think about it. He always knew where we were, though, and He made sure we got exactly what we needed when we needed it—sometimes in spite of us. Now we see Him using all we went through to help other people and we're blessed every time that happens. That's why I can't..."

"So it is survivor guilt!" Jax muttered. Then he looked up in embarrassment. "Did I..."

Ethan was grinning from ear to ear. "Yep, you did, my friend. Right out loud. And you may be right; I may be trying to vindicate my own failings somehow. But whether you believe it or not, I care what happens to you and your family. So do Liz and the Zimmerman's. And God cares most of all, so we wouldn't dare give up. I'm afraid you're stuck with us, whether you like it or not."

He couldn't meet his friend's eyes. "I should have apologized a long time ago, Ethan. Believe it or not, I never used to be so bad-mannered. I'll probably never understand why you care, but you've convinced me." He hesitated. "There's something else..." A longer, even more strained silence. "...something I've never told anyone..."

Ethan said nothing. Anything he said or did now might slam that door again, so he waited patiently until Jax was ready to go on.

"Angel insists there was a 'giant butterfly' that covered her and the boys up when the house fell. She says mommy started to put 'em in the bathroom but the butterfly wouldn't let 'em go in there, and he made 'em hide in the closet. They'd never have survived in that bathroom and I don't have a clue why they ended up where they did, but it's the only place..." He took a shuddering breath and went on. "The boys told the same story at first, but J picked up on the doubts—my doubts—and stopped talking about it, so of course his little brother did, too. My little girl's her mother's daughter, though, and she's never doubted for a minute, or stopped talking about 'her butterfly.'" He gazed into the not-so-distant past, reflexively tearing his napkin to shreds.

"I can't stand to think of that night. When I look at what's left of our house, I can't imagine how they survived. I just keep remembering having to watch it go down with them inside while I was trapped under that tree in the yard. It was..." Another shuddering pause. "Still don't know who showed up to get me free, or how he managed to get that enormous oak off me. Didn't even know how bad my leg was till I tried to get to the house and... and couldn't..." He stared absently, big hands now worrying his coffee spoon, bending it almost double. "I should have been there to protect them then and I'm not even there to protect them now. And I wonder if I'll ever be able to take care of them again. I'm one of the best plumbers around, but plumbers need both legs, and I'm beginning to doubt if my leg will ever be right again."

Ethan listened thoughtfully as Jax talked. Finally he said quietly, "Ya know, Jax, there was a time we thought Liz might never walk again. We'll probably never know how or why she was healed so suddenly when we know others just as deserving who weren't. God says His ways are past finding out and I'm learning, whether we like it or not, most of the time we have no idea why He does what He does. We can be sure it's right, though, and ultimately it will be best for us. I wouldn't pretend to know what the future holds for you, but I do know we're sitting here today because He cares enough about you to bring people to walk alongside you. Marianna's beginning to believe that and it's helping her get through the days. I want you to know I'm praying you'll begin to find that hope, too."

They sat, both lost in their thoughts. Finally Ethan looked at his watch.

"Well, I hate to cut this party short, but I have a bid to finish if I'm gonna get it in by the deadline. I'll bring the car around and meet you at the front door."

The men rode without speaking as they headed north along the partially-restored Range Line. Jax looked up in surprise as his friend suddenly broke the silence.

"Do you need to get back right away, Jax?

He smiled dryly, "Well, my calendar's pretty full, but..."

"I still don't have an estimate on the plumbing for this project," Ethan said. "Would you be interested in taking that on? You can work in the conference room at the office if you feel like it."

Jaxon thought this day couldn't be any more surprising. Panic flooded over him. What if he screwed this up? But this was his world. He could do plumbing estimates in his sleep, and he always brought the jobs in within a percentage point or two.

"Thanks, Ethan. I'd like to give it a shot. And I suddenly feel better than I have in a long time."

3

HOPEFUL ENDINGS

Jax sat in his forlorn little living room, rocking frenetically in Marianna's grandmother's rocker. This chair that had seen three Morris babies soothed and loved and sung to sleep, as well as their mother and her mother before them, had mysteriously been spared when everything around it was demolished. They'd been amazed to find it sitting on top of the mass of debris that had been their home, completely undamaged. Marianna had insisted it was another miracle and maybe there was a God after all. She probably needed to believe that, he'd thought. He loved her enough to try to hide his anger at such a suggestion, but she'd seen right through him, even in her sorrow. She'd never mentioned it again and he couldn't bring himself to talk about it, even though it broke his heart to see how desperately she'd clung to that only remaining connection to her family.

But why was he so upset now? He should be happy. He'd actually spent the afternoon doing work for the first time in nearly two years. Ethan had seemed pleased, even surprised, that he'd finished that big job so fast, but it was pretty much second nature to him. He'd had to make a few calls to update his price lists, but the plumbing estimate had been ready by quitting time.

He'd been happy on the drive home; hopeful for the first time since the tornado that he could carve out some sort of future for his family. Then he'd hobbled into that dreary, empty room and it hit him. There was no one to share this victory with. By his own hand, he was alone.

How had he let things get to this point? His family was splintered even more than that pile of debris that was once their house, and he'd let it happen. No, he'd MADE it happen. What kind of fool does that!

The tears finally came then. Sob after wracking sob, so deep he could hardly breathe. Suddenly he smiled through the tears as his father's voice bellowed into his memory. "Real. Men. Don't. Cry!" How many times had he heard that when he was growing up?

"Well, Pops," he muttered "I'll always love you, but you were wrong. I saw a real man cry today and I want that kind of courage. Maybe even that kind of faith."

That last shocked him. Faith? Where had that come from? There was no such thing. Was there?

"Jaxon? What's happened?"

He stiffened, surprised at the sound of his wife's voice.

"Marianna? What are you... why... are the kids...?"

"They're OK, but what about you, Jax? Something awful must have happened for you to... I've never seen you cry, even when your dad died and I know that just killed you."

She quickly crossed the room to kneel before him, tears gathering in her own eyes.

"Please tell me what's happened. We'll work it out together somehow, I promise."

He reached out a big hand to touch her cheek. "I miss you, Mia. I'm so ashamed I haven't been there for you and the kids. Can you stay and talk a while?"

Her face lit up at the invitation. She'd been prepared for a still-angry Jaxon, or maybe a distant Jaxon, but this new, vulnerable one was a surprise. Maybe all those prayers were working after all.

He pulled her to her feet and led her to the small couch across the room. When they'd moved in they'd laughed that they would absolutely have to remember they needed to be grateful that at least it was clean and new, because it was about the ugliest they'd ever seen. That had been a lifetime ago, he thought wistfully. There'd been no laughter in their household for far too long.

They talked long into the night, not even noticing as the room darkened, content to sit hand in hand in the dim glow of the street light just outside their dingy little window.

Finally she voiced the concern that had brought her here. "I'm worried about J," she said quietly. "He seems so angry all the time and none of us can figure out how to reach him. He needs you, Jax. We need you. Please come to Carthage with us. The Zimmerman's want you to come, too, and they say we can all stay as long as we need to while we figure out where we go from here. Please?"

It was all he could do to get the words out. "I can't yet, Mia. I'm doing better but it's gonna take a little more time. They told me at PT today that if I work hard, my leg should be strong enough before long to hold me up without the cane and they'll release me to drive. I'm gonna work harder than I ever have before and that's a promise." He hesitated, fearful of saying the wrong thing. "You have no idea how much I need to be with you and the kids, for all our sakes, but I have to get rid of this rage first. If I don't, I'll never be what I should be... never be the husband you deserve, or the father the kids need. I was going to call you tomorrow and see if we could work something out so I could see them after school, maybe take them out for burgers or something. Ethan told me about J. I don't want the boys to drop out of soccer. Poor kids don't deserve any more hurt, especially at the hands of their father."

Wordlessly, she pulled his big arm around her and sat, head against his shoulder. Finally, she sighed. "I need to go. Both the boys still have nightmares once in a while, and J will panic if he wakes up and I'm gone. He asked me the other night to promise I wouldn't leave, too." She bit back a second reminder that his family needed him.

The sob shocked her when it came, even after he'd bared his soul in a way she never would have imagined. His arm tightened around her shoulders.

"I'm so sorry, Babe. I start counseling with the guy Ethan's family used day after tomorrow and I promise, as soon as he thinks it's safe we'll find a way to be together. I'll see if Ethan will give me a ride to Carthage tomorrow and if it's OK with the Zimmerman's, maybe I can meet them before we take the kids out. I probably should set up an appointment with their soccer coach, too. Hopefully he'll let them back in if I meet with him and explain why they've missed their games."

Another hug, gentler this time. "Call me when you get back and let me know you're safe?"

The Zimmerman's country home seemed to shout welcome as they drove up the long, winding lane. No wonder Marianna and the kids liked it here. He was surprised to find everyone, including Ethan's wife and kids, in the back yard when they arrived. A celebration of family, they proclaimed. Ethan made introductions all around, and then they immediately put him to work helping grill hot dogs and burgers.

Frank was not at all what he'd expected. Small and bald, he seemed completely unimpressive; though it was evident from the beginning he had some sort of pied-piper effect on the kids. They all adored him, and he seemed to know instinctively how to make each child feel special. It was when he spoke, though, that one saw the real Frank. His voice was as big and booming as his frame was small, and his twinkling eyes seemed to have the ability to look right through one.

Jax had been surprised that by the end of the evening he was almost as comfortable with Frank as he had become with Ethan, and he'd found himself hoping they could eventually be friends. Was that a good sign? For the first time in two years he'd met people he actually wanted to be around. He didn't think he'd ever met anyone like Frank and Ginny Zimmerman, though. They had this ability to make people feel they were doing them a favor, just by accepting their help.

Even so, he soon found himself struggling with the anger he'd hoped was a thing of the past. His family seemed to have begun a whole new life, and he wasn't part of it. He watched the kids playing in the yard with the McConnell "Littles," as Ethan called them, and he was torn between being glad to see them carefree again, even for a little while, and being sad that they'd been able to move on without him. What broke his heart, however, was Angelina. He couldn't stand to think his little Angel was afraid of him, but it took nearly the whole evening for her to finally come to him and sit on his lap. It was no wonder, though. The last time she'd seen him he'd been in a horrible rage, shouting and throwing things.

The evening was both healing and painful. These people made him believe they were genuinely glad he was here, and it was so good to see Marianna laugh again. But it was hard with the boys. He wasn't sure what he'd expected, but he made only a little progress getting past the wall they seemed to have put up. Especially J. The anger he saw hidden in his eyes seemed to mirror his own and it was frightening. He longed to pick him up and hold him close and tell him it would be OK, like he had when he was a baby... to plead with him not to be like his father and let anger take over. Instead, he settled for talking about school and soccer and Ethan's son E.J., who seemed to have become J's new hero. Now almost ten, E.J. was a perfect replica of his burly blond father, brown eyes wise far beyond his years. Though he was only a little older than J, he seemed to have appointed himself protector of both boys, and was surprisingly patient with Eddy Roy's pay-attention-to-me antics.

Jax was surprised when Emma sidled up to him, auburn-gold curls bobbing, coyly informing him that next week she would be six. Big blue eyes sparkling, she said excitedly, "My party is next Saturday. Can you come?" He was trying to decide how to respond to that when a little hand stole into his.

"Daddy, if you come can I come, too?" His heart soared. Strange, he thought, a little girl's birthday party had done what no one else could. He gently lifted his daughter onto his lap and whispered, "I'm pretty sure you're already invited, but I'd love to come too, and we'll have a good time together. OK?"

She turned then, his little Angel once again, and hugged him with all her might. His heart melted. "One step at a time," he warned himself. "Give them time..."

It was obvious the boys were reserving judgement on his promise to come to their school's spring program. He'd certainly earned their distrust, he thought, but he'd be at that program if he had to walk. He grinned. That would be a sight to behold! He could just see himself limping along the highway, leaning on his cane. He didn't notice that that grin was not lost on his wife, nor the circle of friends who'd been praying for him.

He didn't recognize the car that pulled into his drive the following morning. Resolving to be polite this time, even if it was a survey taker or who-knows-what busybody, he shuffled to the wooden railing. Ethan should be here any time and he was ready, so he could surely afford to be courteous. He'd been surprised to realize he was actually looking forward to this first visit to the counselor. "Chris the Counselor," Ethan had joked. Jax hoped he wasn't as young as that sounded...

"Hope you don't mind my giving you a ride, Jax," a big voice boomed.

"Frank!" This was a surprise.

"I had to come to Joplin this morning so I asked Ethan to let me pick you up. Thought it would give us a chance to get to know each other better. I can drop you off wherever you need to go and you can call me when you're finished. OK?"

"Better than OK. I'll sure appreciate the ride and I was hoping we could get to know each other. Not sure I ever said thanks for last night, but it was the best evening I've had in a long time. So... thanks. Let me lock up and I'll be ready to go."

"You can tell me to butt out and I won't be offended, Jax," Frank announced as they drove across town, "but just a word of caution. The first few sessions Ginny and I had with Chris I was convinced it was just making things worse. Guess you have to dredge up all the anger and hurt and confusion and get it into the light before you can begin to work on it."

Jaxon shot a look of surprise at his new friend. "You..."

"I think all of us sooner or later run until things in our lives we just can't handle without help. Ours was having to finally accept that our dream of a house full of kids was never going to happen. At least, not our own kids. Someday I'll tell you the long, boring story of the Zimmerman's.

Ginny and I are praying for patience for you and discernment for Chris. But don't be put off by how he looks. He isn't as young as he seems; and anyway, he's wise far beyond his years." He paused as he pulled to a stop at the entrance of a converted Victorian home in the historic part of town; then added, "It's not easy for us men to open up to anyone, let alone a stranger, but if you ever need to talk to someone who's been there..."

The session had felt awkward, even painful at times, but Jax came away surprisingly relieved. At least he was finally doing something positive.

He was glad Frank suggested a quick lunch before he dropped him off at home. Two hours later he hobbled up his front steps, exhausted but somehow lighter of heart than he'd been in years. He hoped Mia didn't have plans for tonight. Maybe they could take the kids for ice cream.

4

GOOD NEWS/BAD NEWS AND OTHER STORIES

Jaxon thought he'd probably had enough x-rays by now to glow in the dark, but he was grateful Doc had rushed this last set through so they could look at them before he left today. Whatever the verdict was, he needed to move on with his life. Still, he couldn't stifle the fear gnawing at the pit of his stomach as Dr. Jefferson opened the exam room door.

"The good news is," his surgeon announced cheerily, "you can retire that cane whenever you're ready; and by next week, if PT signs off, I should be able to release you to drive."

Jax took a deep breath. Retiring that cane was a big deal, but...

"So, what's the bad news, Doc?"

"I know you well enough by now to know you'd just as soon have it straight, Jax, so here it is. The fact that you can walk at all after the damage your leg sustained is just short of a miracle and if you keep up the rehab, I'm confident you'll be able to lead a normal life. Just not the same life. Your leg, to put it crudely, is held together with rods and screws and baling wire. It will withstand normal activity, maybe even very light sports, but your days of hard labor are a thing of the past."

"But... but I'm a..."

"A plumber," smiled the doctor, "and one of the best. I haven't forgotten what good work you did for us not long ago and frankly, I hate to have to find someone new; but I don't see any way you could do such strenuous work now. If you put your leg through that kind of abuse, you'd be back on a cane permanently in less than five years. I wish I had better news. I know how much your work means to you and I won't presume to know how you feel right now, but I also know you're stronger than you think and you'll figure something out. The city is sponsoring retraining programs for people who aren't able to do the work they did before. I can make a few calls if you like."

He clapped the big man on the shoulder. "God's still in your corner, my friend, and a lot of people are praying for you. If there's anything I can do..."

Somehow he'd gotten out of Doc's office without losing it, but by the time Frank pulled in he could feel that familiar rage boiling up. Sure, God was in his corner! What kind of god took away everything that was important? What good were prayers when the answers—if there were such things—only got worse and worse?

He slid numbly into the car, barely aware of his surroundings. At the look on his face Frank stifled his normal greeting, silently praying for his friend as he put the car into gear.

He roused as Frank pulled to a stop and cut the ignition. Was that a stream in the valley below? Where were they, and how had they gotten here without his even noticing? He looked a question at Frank, who sat calmly regarding him.

"Good place to lob a few rocks or kick some dirt or take a short walk and scream at God. Might help relieve some of that tension. Or," he smiled gently, "we could just talk. Obviously the news isn't good, my friend. How can I help?"

Jax sat looking at big hands that had always been his livelihood. Suddenly they seemed completely useless.

"Dunno," he finally managed. "I know a lot of people have it a lot worse, but... Doc told me I can get rid of the cane any time, but I won't be able to plumb again." He looked up then, the old agony back in his eyes. "That's all I've ever done, Frank. All I ever wanted to do. It's who I am—who my Pops was. I was just starting to build a really good business of my own, and I've always dreamed that someday I'd hand it down to my sons. Pops always said you'll never go hungry if you have a trade..." He paused, then said half under his breath, "Sorry, Pops, but that's the second thing you got wrong..." Frank waited patiently until he was ready to go on. "Doc said he could refer me to a re-training program. That's probably what I'm gonna have to do, but I feel like it's giving up a big chunk of my life."

"Because it is, Jax."

He looked at his friend in surprise. He'd expected some sort of cliché, like, "It's gonna be OK," or "It's for the best," or worst of all, "God knows what you need." Probably all true, he thought, except for the God part, but he was grateful Frank hadn't insulted him with empty platitudes.

"I know I'll have to make the best of it, Frank. It is what it is, but I feel like someone just asked me to step off that cliff blindfolded."

"Pretty dramatic for a plumber," Frank chuckled, "but I'd say that's a pretty good description of where you are right now."

When Jax made no response, he added quietly, "Could I make a suggestion?"

Jax nodded silently.

"Ethan said you did a great job on the estimate you did for him. Seems like that might be a logical first step. You know the business inside and out. Or there's always a need for draftsmen and mechanical engineers. With your experience in the field, that might be an easy transition. And those are just a couple of possibilities. The money might not be quite as good, but you wouldn't find yourself wondering where you go from here when you're fat and fifty-five."

They sat staring solemnly at each other until first Jax and then Frank dissolved in laughter at the mental image of Jaxon James Morris II as a fifty-five-year-old, fat, pot-bellied, former plumber.

"How about coming up for dinner, Jax? Seems like we need to celebrate your liberation from that 'blasted cane,' as you call it, and you need to let Marianna know what the doctor said. You have some decisions to make as a family."

He just nodded again. He already knew better than to object that Ginny might not be ready for company. He'd learned the Zimmerman's were always ready to entertain with great enthusiasm. Besides, it might be easier to keep it together if they were there when he gave his wife the news.

The six friends relaxed on the patio, enjoying the early fall evening. Ginny had called the McConnell's to join them and now they sat, watching the children play hide and seek in the gathering dusk, laughing at Jax's vision of himself as a fat fifty-five year old. Strange, Jax thought. He couldn't remember when he'd felt more peaceful. The news today should have left him restless and frustrated. He had to admit he'd been as furious as ever at first, but Frank's confidence in his future—and Doc's honesty and reassurance—had awakened some sort of hope in him he hadn't even known existed. He smiled, remembering his doctor's hand on his shoulder. He knew he'd meant it when he offered help. He'd become a good friend, even calling Jax at home to check on him a few times. Imagine, Jaxon Morris, plumber; blue-collar worker from Detroit, personal friends with a surgeon. He was beginning to see that the monster that blew away life as they'd known it might have blown them into a life he'd never have dreamed possible. Frank and Ethan and Doc... and Chris... would say it was part of God's plan for them, but he wasn't ready to go that far. If there was a god, he didn't think he liked one that seemed to give good things to some and the worst of things to others. Besides, he couldn't imagine any god he'd ever heard of bothering with all the little problems in this little town, or anywhere else on this miserable earth.

Jax and Marianna sat in her car holding hands, exhausted from hours of talk. And tears. It seemed like lately the tears were just there, ready to escape at the slightest excuse. Strange thing was, it didn't really bother him so much anymore. With apologies to Pops, he thought, sometimes it actually seemed like those tears made him stronger. It was definitely better than being in a rage all the time.

He stole a sideways glance at his wife. What an awesome woman fate had somehow allowed into his life. Doing the right thing at the right time just seemed to come naturally to her. Like casually handing him the keys when they got to the car tonight. He had to admit, it felt good to be behind the wheel again. What was it about driving a car that appealed to a man's ego? He smiled. Jax Morris, philosopher. Former plumber. He wasn't sure he knew this man that seemed to live in his body now. Mostly, though, he kinda liked him. So far.

They'd stayed at the Zimmerman's until the kids were all asleep. He didn't think he could handle more tears or hurt looks, and they couldn't possibly understand why Daddy didn't want to stay with them. If they only knew how much he wished he could, but he was determined to do this right—finally. As soon as Chris thought he was ready they'd be together. Didn't matter whether it was in that beautiful basement apartment in Carthage or the dreary little trailer in FEMA Village—what was left of it—-it would be home. Wordlessly, he pulled his wife to him and gently kissed her forehead.

"Could I go with you tomorrow, Jax? I could pick you up and wait in the car if you don't want me to come in, but..."

Well. He sure didn't see that coming, even though Chris had mentioned... surely he wouldn't have... No. Chris would never violate patient confidentiality. Was Mia feeling the same need for help that he was? Suddenly he was ashamed he hadn't suggested it.

"I-I can't think of anything I'd like more, Honey. Chris actually suggested some joint counseling last time, so I'm sure it's okay, but... I'm so sorry I didn't follow through. I'll call him first thing tomorrow morning. Guess you'll have to drive. I'm not cleared yet, and the new, improved Jax is trying to play by the rules."

She smiled and leaned to kiss him lightly. "I liked the old Jax just fine, thank you very much, but whatever makes you happy..." She sighed. "Guess we'd both better get some sleep if we want to make any sense tomorrow. Out from under that wheel, big boy. I'm taking the power back... for now..."

He met her at the driver's door, wrapping big arms around her to hold her tight. "We're gonna make it, Baby. I promise. And better than ever before. We'd be pretty stupid if we let all this go to waste."

"I love you, Jaxon James Morris, and I'll love you when you're fifty-five, even if you do get fat. Call me in the morning and let me know what time to pick you up."

With another quick kiss and a "Sleep well, my big teddy bear," she was gone, leaving a happy little laugh hanging in the midnight air. It had been so long since she'd called him that. He hugged the endearment close to him as he feel asleep, just as four-year-old Jaxon had hugged the big, fuzzy teddy bear his mother had given him so many years before.

5

TURNING POINTS

The joint counseling had been harder than he'd expected. As they drove for lunch afterward, he couldn't help but wonder if it had been such a good idea. Mia had hardly said a word since they'd gotten in the car and he felt the old familiar fear knot his gut again. He'd hoped he was finally past that. Would he ever get over this uncertainty and sense of failure? How could he be the husband and father his family needed if he was constantly battling insecurity and fear?

Then a slender, delicate hand reached out, lying open palmed on the seat between them, and fear turned to gratitude as he gently closed his own huge one over it. Words weren't really needed right now, were they? They were together and somehow they would deal with whatever came.

He shook his head, remembering that horrific evening almost two and a half years ago. Amazing how just a few minutes could bring such huge change in so many lives. That Sunday in May had been a lot like this day. Beautiful blue skies. Warm sunshine. Green grass and flowers everywhere. He could probably understand how people would want someone to thank for days like that. Problem was, he couldn't trust anything that could let it all be destroyed in such an unspeakable way, in only minutes. He almost envied Mia and their friends. It must be a relief to think there was something bigger than what they could see. He just couldn't do it, though. Life to the Morris clan had always been practical... logical. What you saw was what you got. You made your own way by your own hard work. You paid a fair price for your decisions and you accepted whatever happened because of your actions. How could he believe in something—someone—he couldn't see or hear or begin to figure out? Why would he even want to, when that something was willing to let so many people suffer, even die?

"I'm thinking of getting a part-time job, Jax." His wife's tentative voice shocked him back to the present. "It's only temporary, but I probably need... it might be good... we could use..." She floundered to a stop, dreading his reaction. He'd always been so determined to take care of them, and she didn't want to add to his frustrations, but they really needed the money, and she really needed to do something that felt productive. She loved the basement apartment where she and the kids were living, but caring for it took so little of her creative energy. How could she explain that to this macho man whose identity had always been rooted in his father's definition of manhood?

Finally, he broke the uncomfortable silence. "Are you worried about money, or do you need this for yourself, Babe?"

He was "new and improved," she marveled. The old Jax would never ask a question like that.

"I'm not sure, Bear," she responded, unconsciously slipping into her old term of endearment. "I think probably a little of both. I have a feeling you'll be working before long now that the doctor is ready to release you, though, so it's probably mostly me."

She paused. When he didn't comment she stumbled on, "Ethan needs someone to fill in while one of his office workers is on maternity leave. I could work mornings while Angel is in pre-school. I like the idea that it would only be for a short time, and it would give me a chance to feel like something more than just some kid's mom. Don't get me wrong," she hurried to add. "I love being the kids' mom, but..."

He squeezed her hand. "You don't have to tell me that, Mia. You're the best mom I've ever known. Probably if I was home all the time with three kids I'd be looking for something else to do once in a while, too, so..." He took a deep breath. "I think if that's what you want you should do it. And Ethan had better appreciate what kind of employee he's getting." He grinned. "Just sayin'..."

That wasn't all though, he thought. He tried to wait patiently until she was ready to open up. They were nearly through lunch before she finally spoke her frustration.

"I'm glad you let me go with you today, Bear. I'm impressed with Chris. We probably should set up some sessions for the kids soon, or maybe just some family sessions. Liz told me that really helped them a year or so ago, and I can certainly see how much he's been helping you. I'm truly thankful for that; but I guess I was expecting him to say it's time to get us all back together, and I'm disappointed. I miss you so much, Jax. I just want our family back."

He didn't dare look at her. He was not going to embarrass them both by losing it right here in public. Guess he just wasn't quite the man his friend Ethan was, he smiled grimly to himself.

"I do, too, Baby," he mumbled into the now-frayed napkin on his lap. "You can't possibly know how much; but I'm learning to trust Chris's judgment so..." Finally he looked up, eyes swimming. "Maybe we should set up a counseling time just for you. You've carried such a heavy load for so long, Mia, and mostly by yourself. It's really helped me to talk to someone outside of it all, much as I hate to admit it. How about I call him right now? You don't have to tell me when you go or what you talk about unless you want to."

It had proven to be a turning point. The day became one of the most pleasant they'd had in a very long time. Jax had enthusiastically gone back to Carthage with her and they'd spent the afternoon on the sun-drenched patio, playing tea party with Angel until she had fallen asleep in her father's arms, then chatting and laughing about everything and nothing.

Eddy Roy was the first to notice him there when the boys got home from school, nearly bowling him over in his excitement.

"Dad! You're here! Are you gonna stay? Can we play catch? Can I show you my homework? Can we go out for burgers and ice cream? J, look, Dad's here..."

They laughed as Jax theatrically fell to the ground, overwhelmed by his son's onslaught.

"Hey, one thing at a time. Yes, I'm gonna stay till you go to bed. Yes, we can play catch, or anything else you want. Yes, I absolutely want to see your homework. Yes, we can go out for burgers but we'll have to talk to Mom about the ice cream. And yes, yes, yes, I really, really, really miss you guys."

His older son stood frozen, a panoply of emotions playing across his face. The first flush of excitement and joy had been quickly swallowed up by fear and anger and uncertainty. Jax sat up, wordlessly holding out his arms. "J?" It was a risk. He wasn't sure what he'd do if J refused his invitation, but he'd do whatever it took to help his son begin trusting his dad again.

Suddenly Jaxon James Morris III was in his father's arms, a broken little boy who'd tried too hard to be the man in the family, sobbing and clinging to him as if he'd never let go. Jax held him close, his own tears falling freely, whispering love and reassurance, finally able to promise it would all be OK; that they'd all be together soon. It never occurred to him to tell his son that real men don't cry.

6

HARD TRUTHS

Jax was an early riser. Years of trying to get as much hard work in before the day got too hot had only enhanced his early-morning nature. Today, though, was exceptional. He woke long before dawn and could not stay in bed. He showered and dressed quickly and took his coffee to the little front stoop to watch the sun come up. He breathed in the fresh morning air and smiled. Today he would begin looking for work, for the first time in two years.

He glanced at the SUV in the drive. He still couldn't believe how casually Ethan had handed him the keys. Then he'd found the stack of slacks and shirts and jackets on the front seat, and well, he'd never known anyone like these people. He'd loved his life before, still missed the good-natured rivalry and boisterousness of myriad construction sites. But this was a whole new world. These people seemed to live like anything they owned somehow belonged to whoever needed it. If this really was what Christianity was all about, he could almost see the appeal of it.

Life lately had been pretty much a whirlwind of good things. Was it actually only last week that Doc had smilingly handed him the release to drive and return to work? He'd grinned at the stern instructions that followed: "Stay away from hard labor. Stay with your PT. And by all means, stay in touch." He'd been surprised that he had such mixed feelings. He'd really miss this likeable man—he'd seen him through some very hard times the past two years.

He probably should start with some of the construction sites first. Hopefully, that might give him some idea where to head next. He'd promised Ethan he'd call a little before noon. He was gratified that these two busy, successful men wanted to take him to lunch. They said it was to celebrate, but he sort of thought it might be more about giving him some reinforcement. Job hunting was such a humbling experience, even in the best of circumstances.

Humbling didn't even begin to describe his day, he thought wearily as he climbed his bleak wooden steps that evening. He was exhausted to the bone, almost too tired to heat the dinner Mia had left for him in the fridge. She'd easily read him when she called. She wouldn't wear him out with questions, she'd said cheerfully. Just wanted to remind him that there were lots of people praying for him and she and the kids loved him and were very, very proud of him. Bless her, he'd thought. She made him believe every word.

In spite of his best efforts, by the end of the week his excitement at being back in the field had been buried under mountains of discouragement and rejection. Jobs in the area were far from being back at normal levels, and many younger, less restricted applicants were still out there.

As he stumbled into his bedroom Friday evening, he was actually glad to only get his wife's voicemail. "Hey, Baby," he said wearily. "I'm fine but exhausted. Going right to bed. Tomorrow's another day. We should do something with the kids. Call you in the morning. Love you."

"God, does it have to be so hard?" he blurted as he pulled the covers over his shoulders. God? Where had that come from? Oh well, he was desperate enough to try anything at this point. He closed his eyes. (Wasn't that what you were supposed to do?) He guessed he probably should get down on his knees or something, but if there really was a God like Ethan described, maybe He'd understand how exhausted he was.

"God, if you really exist, and you really care like Mia thinks you do, I need to know. I'm finding out I'm not nearly as good as I always believed and I guess I need a lot of help, so-o-o, here I am..."

Weird, he thought. Nothing had really changed. There'd been no answer that he knew of—certainly no voice out of the blue or light from the sky. He was still as tired as ever; but that little prayer (if that's what it was) had somehow made him feel more at peace.

He was asleep by the time his head hit the pillow.

"Daddy, will you go to Sunday School with me tomorrow? My teacher's really nice and she tells such good stories and she said she'd be bery glad to get to meet you and I really, really, really want you to go. Will you?"

They'd just finished grilling hot dogs at the park, and the boys were anxiously waiting for Mom's OK to go to the playground when his daughter's question surprised them all. Well, he'd known he'd have to deal with it sooner or later.

He shot a look at his wife. She sat quietly at the picnic table, carefully inspecting her nails, seemingly in another universe. A lot of help she was. He was surprised neither of the boys had joined in their sister's invitation. Were they afraid he'd embarrass them in front of their new friends? And just why didn't his wife ever ask him to go with her? What, or who, was there that she didn't want him to see?

Stop! he cautioned himself sternly. Where in the world had those ridiculous thoughts come from? His boys were always proud to show him off, and his wife was completely faithful in every way. Good thing some thoughts never saw the light of day, he thought ruefully, but even having them confused and shamed him.

"Ya know what, Princess?" he heard himself say. "I think it's time we made this church thing a family thing. When do I need to pick you up, Mommy? We'll all go together."

Three heads came up at that. Three pairs of brown eyes regarded him with shock. Church! He realized he was just about as shocked as they were. What had he just done? Then the look in his wife's eyes wrapped around his heart as his daughter's little arms wrapped around his neck, and he decided it was a very small price to pay for the joy he saw there.

It wasn't nearly as bad as he'd expected. People had been friendly, glad to meet Marianna's husband (or the kids' dad), but no one acted like there was anything strange about his being there. He'd actually enjoyed the upbeat music, and the speaker had been nothing like the shouting, podium-pounding stereotype he'd always imagined. In fact, he'd found himself intrigued with the message of love and mercy he'd heard. He even remembered some of the things the man said, especially about forgiveness. He'd sure needed a lot of that lately.

Now the Morris's sat at a long table at their favorite restaurant, chatting comfortably with Liz and Ethan and the Zimmerman's. Jax had thought he didn't want to talk about his job search or today's daunting venture into the church world, but he suddenly found himself sharing both without reservation. These were his friends, after all. In fact, he finally realized, they seemed almost like family. Why had he been so afraid to trust them?

Now Frank was recounting his own panic and awkwardness the first time he'd gone to church with Ginny, laughing with the rest of them when she interjected, "You think *you* were nervous!"

Jax was shocked to hear that religion had never been a part of Frank's background, either. His family had proudly proclaimed themselves secular Jews. Even so, when their son began dating a Christian they'd declared it a betrayal of his heritage. He'd never been sure, he smiled, whether he fell in love with Ginny first, or Jesus, but he was glad he'd made the commitment to both and he'd never looked back. His parents had eventually forgiven them, Ginny added. Now her parents-in-law laughed that they were "completed Jews" and they would tell you they were about the happiest Christians you could find. And that wasn't all. Five years ago Frank had joyfully baptized his last sibling into Christ.

Well, thought Jax, this was a world he still couldn't quite grasp, but he wanted to know more. Maybe he was beginning to like it in spite of himself.

The next two weeks were brutal. Doors seemed to close at every turn. He came to dread evenings alone in his little trailer; struggled mightily to control his rising fear and anger; tried his best to hide it from those he loved; went for long walks and more counseling; and finally, exhausted, fell on his knees in his lonely room, again crying out to the God he still wasn't sure existed.

"God, I still don't know if you're there or not. It didn't seem like you answered last time, unless... well, maybe it could have been you that... something sure made me feel better, so..." He paused for a steadying breath. "Anyway, I know I need help and I just don't have anywhere left to go. I'm sure I don't have any right to ask but I don't know what else to do. I always thought I could handle about anything, but..." He sighed. "Frank and Ethan seem so sure about you... keep insisting you care about me. Right now, I'd like to believe that's true. If it is, would you show me somehow? Could you give me a sign or something? Anything. Please?" What else should he say? "Thank you," he finished lamely, then floundered to a stop, feeling foolish about talking into an empty room like there was really someone there.

"The Bible."

"Wh-what?" He whirled, certain someone had spoken. But he was alone, as usual. It had to be his imagination.

"The Bible." There it was again. He felt his breath quicken, his pulse race. What was going on? He must be losing it for sure. Where had that thought come from? They'd never owned a Bible and he wouldn't even know where to find one, especially in the middle of the night. Suddenly, his mind's eye clearly saw it. A black Bible, lying in a big cardboard box. That's right! There'd been one in that Thanksgiving box the McConnell's had left them a couple lifetimes ago. He'd ordered Marianna to throw it away, but down deep he'd known she was too soft-hearted to throw away a gift, even if it was from strangers. Hopefully she'd kept it somewhere. Suddenly it was incredibly important to find that Bible. Now where...

Twenty minutes later he'd searched every inch of the prefabricated box that was his home. It had to be here somewhere but he wasn't about to call Marianna to ask if she'd seen it. Maybe she'd taken it back to Carthage with her. She certainly would never expect Jax to need it. Finally he sank to the couch, defeated, staring out the window, wondering why it seemed so urgent. Then a dark object under the chair in the corner caught his eye.

Of course! Angelina. She'd loved books since she was old enough to sit up. She'd happily crawl into a corner and thumb through any book she could find. In happier days they'd laughed that she was the only child they knew who hoarded books like most kids hoarded candy. Excitedly he retrieved the now-slightly-dog-eared book and returned to the couch.

So, where in the world should he start? He shrugged. The beginning was probably a good place. "In the beginning God created..." Hm-m-m. He'd heard a lot of arguments about how the world started, but he'd never known that was how the Bible started. After a few chapters, he paused. Interesting history, he thought with surprise, but somehow it didn't seem like that was what he needed right now. Idly, he opened the book at random. "In the beginning was the Word, and the Word was with God and the Word was God." That was strange! He'd turned to the middle of the book, and this chapter started "in the beginning," too. Well, it was nice poetry but completely confusing. For some reason, though, he couldn't stop reading.

An hour later he laid the Bible down, thoughts whirling. He still couldn't quite grasp how this Jesus Christ could be "the Word" and "God" and "with God" all at the same time, but the man's prayer for His disciples in the middle of that first section had somehow touched something deep down inside him anyway. And then when he'd read it was also a prayer for everyone yet to come, he couldn't deny the strange longing he was beginning to feel. The next section, "Acts," was sort of like reading an adventure novel. He was amazed at everything Jesus' followers had been willing to go through just because they believed in Him. Then came "Romans." That one seemed pretty much practical and straightforward—something he could get his teeth into. He thought he might have liked this Paul guy. From what Jax could tell, he didn't mess around; just told it like it was.

Could this all be true? How could anyone have the kind of faith those men he'd been reading about had seemed to? Frank and Ethan did, too, he thought wistfully, and from what he'd seen, so did Ginny and Liz.

Frank answered his phone on the first ring, obviously alarmed at such a late call.

"Frank, I'm sorry. I know it's late, but could you possibly come down? I've already called Ethan and he's on his way. I've got to... I'm not sure... I think God... I just need to talk..."

They were both there in record time. Must have broken speed limits all the way, thought Jax, and they didn't waste time asking questions. Just sat listening intently, coffee cups in hand, as Jax described his evening, from the first awkward prayer to his growing understanding of what he was reading to the sudden overwhelming need to find this God he'd denied his whole life. Their prayers for him that night were, for the first time in his life, welcome. They left with the rising sun, agreeing to meet once a week to study with him. In the meantime, he would keep reading and keep asking questions. And, he promised, he'd try to keep believing God really was helping him in this miserable journey.

7

NEW REALITIES, NEW LIFE

"No! No no noooo!"

A terrified little voice once again shattered the night. Marianna was instantly awake. It was becoming an almost nightly occurrence. Jax laid his hand on his wife's arm.

"I'll go. This is something J and I need to work through together. Hopefully he hasn't wakened the other two."

He found his firstborn son sitting rigidly upright in bed, glassy eyes staring at unseen horrors.

"J, Dad's here," he whispered reassuringly. He gently picked him up, blanket and all, but the little boy stiffened in his arms, still fighting the terror that seemed to await him each night. He wrapped the blanket around the struggling boy and carried him into the moon-washed living room of the basement apartment that had, as of a few months ago, finally become his home.

"J," he whispered again. "Dad's here. You're safe."

He settled into the soft chair in the corner, holding him gently but firmly, whispering "Dad's here" over and over until he felt him relax in his arms. Finally, slowly, little arms stole around his neck; then held on tightly as the tears came.

"Daddy. I was so scared, Daddy," he sobbed into his father's shoulder. "It was so dark and loud and then the house fell down and we couldn't get out and... and... the butterfly guy was there and he told us not to be afraid and Angel never was but I was... I was so scared." He gulped a shallow breath and hurried on, "I couldn't help it. I was so scared 'cause I knew Angel and Eddy and Mommy needed help and I couldn't move and I didn't know where you were and I couldn't figure out how to help 'em..." His words drifted off and Jax sat silently, hoping he might sleep now, but the heartrending litany began again. "Now when I go to sleep I dream it's coming again. Mr. Chris says the dreams are gonna go away. He says to be sure and tell you or Mommy whenever I'm scared or sad. He said my butterfly guy's still taking care of me even if I can't see him anymore."

Suddenly the little head came up, pleading brown eyes looking into his father's. "Daddy, do you think my butterfly guy was my very own angel? That's what Mr. Chris says, but... do you think there really are angels?"

Wow. Jax wasn't sure he was ready for this conversation any time, especially in the middle of the night. Well, Chris says be honest with the kids about things like this so...

He tousled his son's dark hair. "Y'know, buddy, I don't really know. I'm still getting to know about God and Jesus and the Bible and all that stuff, but it sure seems like something was taking care of us. It was a really scary time, wasn't it; but something, or someone, made sure you kids and Mommy were where you wouldn't get hurt." He stopped, reliving that night again; this time from a different perspective. "And," he said thoughtfully, "I don't know anyone strong enough to lift that humongous tree that fell on me all by himself, but some guy did. I don't know how he got me out from under it, either, but he did. And then I just didn't see him anymore." He gave his son a quick wink. "Ya think your angel might have had a buddy out there to help me that night?"

Solemn brown eyes considered him wordlessly until finally an exhausted little boy sighed and leaned his head against his father. At last he slept.

Jax sat, unwilling to let him go; praying that the God he was beginning to believe was there would help them through this latest battle to heal their family.

Marianna found them there the next morning, peacefully sleeping as the bright morning sun warmed the room.

"I dunno, Babe," Jax said pensively. "I thought getting us all back together would help the kids, but they actually seem worse since I've been here. J's having nightmares every night, Angel's having tantrums for the first time ever, and Eddy Roy's withdrawn into some little world of his own. I know Chris says to give them time, they're still trying to deal with all the changes, probably still afraid I'm gonna leave again, but it's just killing me. I can't stand to see them in such turmoil." Anguished eyes full of remorse and guilt came up to meet his wife's. "I don't know how you did it all those months, Mia. How can you keep from hating me? I don't think I can ever forgive myself for leaving you to deal with it by yourself. I'm so sorry."

She said nothing. Just moved to stand behind his chair and slip her arms around him as she often did, leaning her cheek against his hair.

Finally, with a strained little chuckle, he went on, "I never thought I'd ever even think such a thing, let alone say it, but I want to believe there's a God. I want to know He's good and intends for this to all work out somehow but it seems like the more I try to believe and the harder I try to make things right, the worse things get. I have to be honest. I'm beginning to wonder if it's worth it. Isn't believing in God supposed to make your life better?"

"I really think it does," she said hesitantly. "When I see how the McConnell's and Zimmerman's live, and some of the other people we've met at church, there's a big difference. It doesn't have anything to do with jobs or nice houses or money or stuff, though. It's... it's deeper than that. I actually think *we're* better somehow, even with all that's happening right now. Before the tornado I always thought we had one of the happiest families around; but it still seemed like something was missing. I just couldn't figure out what. Now, since I've started studying the Bible and praying and learning more about Jesus, it's sort of like a hole I didn't even know was there is being filled."

She moved back to her chair at the table and took his hands. He waited uncomfortably, wondering what was coming next.

"Honey, I don't want to rush anything, or make you feel pressured in any way, but I think I'm ready to 'go all in,' as Ethan calls it."

"What, exactly, does that mean?" he asked guardedly.

"It means, exactly, that I want to be a Christian."

"I, uh... I'm... not..."

"I know you're not ready to make that kind of decision, Jax, and that's OK. I'm praying you will soon. Being around Liz and Ethan's family makes me want to raise our kids the way they're raising theirs. It seems like Jesus is always the center of everything for them. I know it doesn't mean there won't be problems; or that sooner or later one of them won't make some bad choices. I just want ours to grow up in a home where Jesus lives, too. But please don't feel pressured, Bear. Something that important has to be all yours, between you and the Lord first. I just wanted you to know I'm going to make a commitment this Sunday. I didn't want it to take you by surprise."

He *was* surprised, he thought, but he guessed he shouldn't be. He'd seen enough change in Mia that he should have known it was only a matter of time. Strange thing was, though, he was actually glad. Maybe there'd been some change in him, too.

He could tell she was nervous. She was trying her best to hide it, but those frequent deep breaths told him all he needed to know. She squeezed his hand gratefully when he reached out and took hers.

The sermon seemed to be directed right at them. It was probably exactly what Mia needed to confirm her decision, he thought, but it was the effect it was having on him that left him stunned. He remembered Liz laughing that God had a way of making sure the people He loved got just what they needed at just the right time. Could that be true? Was God really like that? It sounded so personal. Would a god big enough to create the heavens and the earth—he'd pretty well gotten past his doubts about that—actually bother with the little details of people's lives? As much as he still struggled with the idea, wasn't that what he'd seen happening during the tornado? And ever since?

Mia took a deep breath and gently freed her hand from his. It was time! She stepped into the aisle.

And then he knew. This time was for him, too. He stepped into the aisle beside her and, hand in hand, they walked forward into new life.

8

FRESH HOPE

"I have an appointment with the re-training people next Monday, guys. Problem is I don't have a clue what direction I should go. I'm hoping part of what they do is help people figure that out."

The three men had just finished their Friday Bible study and the talk had turned to Jax's job search. He was trying his best to be enthusiastic—at least optimistic—but these friends of his could see right through him. They knew he was still struggling.

"I've accepted that I can't physically do plumbing anymore, but construction is in my blood. I've dreamed of handing down a business to my sons since I was a kid. That was my Pops' dream, too, and I'm still having a hard time turning loose of it. Besides, I just can't see myself working inside in some factory or store or sitting at some desk for the rest of my life. I appreciated the temp job at the Habitat Restore, but frankly, it drove me nuts. I keep thinking surely there's something..."

He paused, finally noticing the smiles on his friends' faces. "OK, guys, what's going on?" He tried to put a more cheerful face on his frustration. "Why the goofy smiles? I'm dyin' here and spillin' my guts and you're sittin' here grinnin'?"

Ethan methodically stacked their Bibles and notebooks and pushed them to the center of the table. "We may have another option for you, my friend, but it will be pretty risky for a while."

Jax couldn't help but laugh. What in his life had *not* been risky the past two and a half years? "OK, I'm hooked. What's going on?"

"It looks like construction is going to be big in this area for quite a while, so Frank's thinking about adding a construction division to his architectural firm. I've really enjoyed being back in the field since the tornado and I've felt like God was pulling me in that direction, too, so we're thinking about forming a partnership. I ran a small construction company for several years before I started my accounting firm, so we both think I'm pretty well equipped to develop the building side while Frank stays with the architectural. Starting a new business is always a risk, though, and there's certainly a chance we could fail. Here's where you come in. We're gonna need a good field supervisor. Everything we've seen tells us you definitely have that kind of potential; but you'd have to be willing to start small—mostly inside—helping do estimates and setting up the teams until we get some jobs going." Jax grinned at the emphasis on "inside." They knew him too well.

"There are no guarantees for any of us," Frank added. "We've agreed if this doesn't work, we'll end it sooner rather than later, and as friends. If it turns out you don't like the job, or it doesn't like you, we'll call it good and help you find something else. We'll understand if you need some time to pray about it. In fact, you probably should..."

"Are you kidding? I *have* been praying about it. At least about the right job. Looks to me like this is God's answer. When do we start?" He looked down at the stack of books, a little embarrassed. "OK, that was a little hasty. I *will* take some time to pray about it, and to talk to Mia. It's her life, too, and she needs to feel OK about it. Besides," he said with a little grin, "my wife has more wisdom in her little finger than the three of us put together."

His new employers would be surprised sometime in the future to learn that their warning that he would have to measure up was the reassurance he needed that this was the real thing, not just more charity. Jaxon James Morris II was grateful for any chance he was given to work, but he was more than ready to get back to carrying his own weight once more.

Finally it was spring again, and life for the Morris family had settled into a predictable rhythm. Jaxon awoke each morning more excited than the day before about the opportunities his new job offered. He wondered now why he'd clung so stubbornly to life as he'd believed it had to be. His position as construction supervisor for the firm of McConnell Zimmerman seemed designed explicitly for him. Organizing multiple projects from his office in the McConnell Building and then overseeing them in the field was more satisfying than he could have imagined. He relished the everyday challenge of learning new things and meeting new demands.

Marianna's days were a dance of soccer matches, birthday parties, swimming and music lessons, play dates and all the daily demands of three children under nine. That in itself would have been enough, but now her days also included sub-contractor meetings and expeditions to flooring and paint stores and visits to appliance centers. And soon she would add furniture shopping to that list.

J and Angelina seemed to be flourishing. Night terrors and tantrums and separation anxieties seemed to be a thing of the past and they'd embraced their new world with delight, spending hours by the pond in the little valley at the back of the Zimmerman yard, excitedly counting the days until the next Bible class in Frank and Ginny's shady back yard. The weekly lessons they'd offered neighborhood kids for years were remarkably creative and fun and this year they'd proven to be just what was needed to help banish the last vestiges of trauma the tornado had left behind. Liz brought E.J. and Emma for the class each week and often in between to play; and both E.J. and J went out of their way to include Eddy Roy.

Still, though he tried his best to be as carefree as the other kids, the little boy seemed to be struggling. Shadows behind eyes that were a little too quick to seek approval seemed to deepen each

43

day, and neither his parents nor Counselor Chris could break through the barriers he'd erected.

That his father didn't see it coming could be excused. After all, his days were filled with demands from every quarter. Even weekends were often not his own. That he needed peace and order the evenings he managed to be home was understandable, and any woman who loved her husband as much as Marianna did would do her best to meet that need.

But her mother's heart saw, and knew that sooner or later the barrier would have to break. What she did not know was why. What troubled her youngest son, and why could she not find the key to unlock his sadness? Nights were often spent alone on her knees, desperately seeking wisdom and discernment. But even she could not have expected what was to come.

9

CHASING SHADOWS

"Jax. I'm so sorry to bother you. I know this project is at a crucial point, but..." His heart sank. Mia never called him at work.

"What's wrong, Babe? What's happened?"

"We're on the way to the hospital—it's gonna be OK—but I think we need you here." She was trying to sound calm, but Jax could feel the tension in her voice.

"Hospital! Who... what... Mia, what's going on?"

"It's Eddy Roy, Jax. I'm sure his leg is broken. He's being so brave but he needs his daddy, and frankly, so does his mommy."

"I'll meet you there, Babe. You're right. It's gonna be OK." He didn't waste time asking any more questions.

"Please, God," he implored as he sprinted for his car. "Not Eddy Roy. You know he's the only one who still hasn't gotten over the tornado. He's such a fragile little guy, in spite of how sturdy he looks. Why would You let him go through even more suffering?"

He fumbled for his buzzing phone, breathing a small sigh of relief when he heard Ethan's voice.

"Jax, Liz just called. She was with Marianna when they found Eddy and she's on the way to the hospital now. Ginny has the kids. Don't worry about things here; we're covered. Do you need me to come?"

"Thanks, brother. Not sure at this point. Maybe just be sure things are OK on the job. I don't think I even told anyone I was leaving, so..." He struggled to keep his voice from breaking. "Sorry, I just..."

"Hey. I'd have done the same thing. When your family needs you, you go. I know Liz will keep me posted on Eddy Roy and Marianna, but I'm going to want to know how *you're* doing, so give me a call when you have time to catch your breath. You know we're all praying."

He was gone before Jax could respond. Someday he hoped he could tell these people how much they had come to mean to his family, and to him.

He got to the ER just as Doc Jefferson was walking into the room. What were the odds this man would be on call today, he thought gratefully. His friend gave him a quick squeeze on the shoulder and then turned to his little patient.

"Well, young man, let's see what we can do to make you feel better. I'm Dr. Jefferson, but since your dad and I are such good friends, you can call me Doc. OK?"

Eddy Roy's eyes widened at that, but he simply nodded mutely. Jax thought his heart would break. His son was white as a ghost and obviously in agony, but his eyes were lifeless, his face almost expressionless. How could any seven-year-old boy be in so much pain without crying? He glanced at Marianna. She met his questioning look with her own.

"Well, Eddy, my man," the doctor was saying, "we're gonna take you to get pictures of that leg and we'll have you all fixed up before you know it. Mom and Dad can come with you. Any questions?"

Again that stoic look and a slight shake of the head. Jax was beginning to worry there was more going on here than a broken leg.

They returned from x-ray to a waiting room full of people. Not only had Frank and Ethan gotten there in record time, but it looked like half their Sunday morning Bible class was there, too. They'd been members of this church nearly a year, Jax reflected, and he still couldn't get used to the way these people took care of each other.

"Doc says our little man is lucky," Jax reported. He's sure there are no injuries besides his leg. It's broken in two places, but they both look like clean breaks and at his age it should all heal without any hardware. They'll probably keep him here a few days after surgery, and then he's gonna be laid up for a while, so you can pray we'll find ways to keep him occupied—and his mother sane. Thank God school's already out. He'll have the whole summer to recover. He's probably gonna be pretty unhappy about missing sports and swimming, but Doc says he expects him to be fine by next fall, so..." he stopped to catch his breath, "it could have been worse."

No one mentioned what each one there was thinking. It *had* been worse for Eddy Roy's father.

The wait had seemed interminable, even though the waiting room had been a beehive of well-wishers since they'd gotten there. Eventually it began feeling chaotic, Liz had realized, so she'd quietly stepped in, fielding calls and welcoming the latest arrivals.

"Jax, why don't you take Marianna to get something to eat?" Frank suggested. "Looks to me like she's beginning to run out of steam. We'll hold down the fort here, and they'll page you if Doc comes out before you get back."

Typical Frank and Liz, Jax thought gratefully. Having everyone there had made the waiting easier, but as much as they appreciated all the support and prayers, they could use a little alone time now. He could tell it had been almost more than Marianna could handle to keep having to bring newcomers up to date.

The kids had been begging to have a picnic at the site of their new house, she'd told them, and since the workers wouldn't be there today she'd finally agreed to take them. Thank God that on a last-minute whim she'd invited Liz and the kids to go along. She shuddered to think how she would have managed if they'd been there alone.

She wasn't sure how long Eddy Roy had been gone when she noticed he wasn't with the other kids, but they'd immediately begun searching. It had felt like an eternity, but when they couldn't find him on the grounds or around the machinery she'd decided to search the basement. She'd found him there, lying on the concrete floor. At first she'd been terrified he might have hit his head. He never called out for help, and he hadn't said a word since they found him. Doc assured them he was pretty sure it was just emotional trauma. All the tests showed there was no head injury. They'd keep a close watch and refer him for counseling if he needed it, but he expected Eddy would come around in just a few days.

They were relieved the cafeteria was quiet at this time of day. At her husband's gentle urging, Marianna managed a few bites of who-knew-what; tried mightily to be cheerful for his sake; then sank into a dejected contemplation of her nearly-full plate. He tried to wait patiently for her to work through her thoughts.

Finally it came. "I should have watched him closer, Jax. I can't believe I took them into a construction site. Just because it's ours doesn't mean there aren't dangers there. I've been so looking forward to finally having a place where we could all feel safe again, and now they may only think of that terrible, dark basement where Eddy could have died." Tears slipped silently down her face. "He's only a little boy, Jax. He's only a little, vulnerable boy and I'm his mother and I didn't protect him."

He was stunned. He leaned across the small round table to grab her hands. "Mia, Honey, look at me! You can't blame yourself. You know trying to keep track of little boys is like herding cats. Accidents are just gonna happen. The last thing Eddy needs is an anxious, over-protective mother. Please don't beat yourself up for something no one could have predicted. We need you, Babe. The kids and I need you strong and reminding us God is in control."

He watched shock, then anger, then sorrow play across her face. "Jax! You're so right. This is not about me! Feeling sorry for myself isn't going to help any of us, especially the kids, and they're all traumatized. Angel was with Liz and Emma when we found Eddy so she didn't see him until they put him in the ambulance, but Liz says she cried and cried when we left. J was the first one to find him, though, and when he saw him at the bottom of that ladder he was terrified. And you know how E.J. is. I could tell he was already feeling like he should have somehow kept Eddy from getting in trouble. We need to call the kids right now. They need to know their brother is OK."

He was dialing Ginny's number before she finished speaking.

Doc met them in the hall as they came back to the waiting room. "He's doing great. It couldn't have gone better. As I expected, the breaks were clean, so his leg should heal without any complications. He'll be in a cast for several months, but they'll be progressively smaller and lighter over time. He'll be in recovery for a while yet but we'll make sure you're there when he starts waking up so you'll be the first faces he sees." He clapped Jaxon on the shoulder and gave Marianna a quick hug as he turned to leave; then abruptly turned back. "Marianna, if you're like most moms, you're probably blaming yourself. Don't do that. Just keep in mind that boys have a wonderful ability to get themselves in trouble—it's part of our DNA—so cut yourself and your son some slack." He didn't have time to ask why his friends found that caution funny

It had been an exhausting week. It had taken some gentle arm twisting and a reminder that J and Angel needed their mom, too; but finally on the third day, Marianna had agreed to go home and let Jax spend the night. She had to admit seeing the other kids and getting a good night's rest had been a healing time for her.

Now it was the fourth day of her little boy's recovery. She was back, but Eddy Roy had still not spoken a word. His favorite story and several favorite songs had brought no response at all and she'd gone to sleep by his bed with a fearful, heavy heart.

"Mo-o-om-m?"

She smiled in her sleep. It was always so good to hear that sweet little voice, even in the middle of... She came upright, wide awake. Praying it hadn't been a dream, she reminded herself not to over-react.

"Did you call me, Honey? Are you hurting?"

Suddenly, heart-rending sobs filled the dim room. "It-it was a-all my f-fa-a-ult. I didn't mind Daddy and now he's mad and you're m-mad and God's p-prob'ly mad at me, t-to-o-o. Please d-don't be mad, M-mommy. I'm s-s-sorry-y-y..."

She wrapped her arms around the sobbing little boy, careful not to disturb the tension bar that held his leg above the bed.

"Oh my Little Bear. Don't cry. Nobody's mad at you and God loves us all so, so much, even when things *are* our fault. But why do you think that? Can you tell me what happened?"

Now the little boy who had been so silent and stoic could not stop talking and sobbing.

"I just wanted to show Daddy I was big enough to help. I was gonna go down and sweep out the basement so he'd be proud of me, too."

Uh-oh. Was this what had been going on in that troubled little heart the last few months? Had they been looking in the wrong places for answers?

Before she could respond, he caught his breath and rushed on. "I wish I didn't get on that ladder. He told me not to and now he'll never... Will you tell him not to be mad? Could you tell my daddy I'm sorry?"

She thought her heart would shatter. She shot a silent appeal to her own Father. "You promise wisdom when we ask for it, Lord, and I sure need it now. How do I walk this baby through this without piling guilt on top of injury and still make sure I don't discourage his sense of responsibility?"

Then she found herself saying gently, "I promise he's not mad at you. We're both just sad you're hurt and glad it wasn't worse. I think you do need to say 'sorry' to Daddy because you didn't mind, but he should hear it from you. I'll stay when he gets here in the morning while you tell him, though. OK?"

Once again he nodded mutely, but finally his eyes were alive. With relief. And hope.

Jax had been coming for breakfast with them in the hospital room before he went to work each day, but for some reason he'd felt an urgency to allow a little extra time this morning. The room was still quiet and dark when he got there. Mia stopped him at the door with a finger to her lips; then slipped into the hall for a quick update before they quietly approached the sleeping boy's bed.

He gently brushed the thick, dark hair back from his son's forehead. What was it women sometimes called their daughters? Mini-me? Yep. This little guy was a pretty good copy of him, and his own Pops before him. Before the storm had blown them all away, they used to marvel that they could hardly tell Eddy's baby pictures from his grandfather's.

The little boy stirred and opened his eyes. "Daddy!" He hesitated only a second before he anxiously reached out. The tears came again as he buried his face in his father's shoulder, "I'm so sorry Daddy." Then the words came in a rush, "Mommy-said-you're-not-mad-and-God's-not-either-but-I-would-be-if-my-kid-got-hurt-'cause-he-didn't-mind." A quick breath then, before a dejected lament. "I wish I'd minded you. I promise I'll be better..."

Jax held him close until the sobs ended. Finally, he pulled back enough to take his son's tear-stained face in his big hands.

"I'm not mad, Son. You're right that you should have minded and I'm so sorry you got hurt, but I'm very proud of you for telling the truth." He added, almost as an afterthought, "I bet God's proud of you, too."

Relief and joy washed over the little face that mirrored his own. "You are? You do?"

He laughed. "I am and I do. We need to talk more when you're well. I want to know why you thought you had to do something to earn my love—and God's—but for right now I want you to work hard at believing you already have it and even harder at getting better. Can you promise me you will? We all want to see that fun-lovin' Eddy smile again."

It was almost as if someone had flipped a switch. Eddy Roy was once again a cheerful, talkative little boy; eager to do everything he was told. But his mother still sometimes saw a shadow behind those brown eyes, and it seemed to her he was just a little too eager to please.

"Wow, Ed! Cool wheels!" envied his big brother.

Somehow Doc had managed to send his "favorite patient" home with a state-of-the-art lightweight wheel chair that would see him through until he graduated to crutches.

His brother and sister had spent the day making "Welcome Home" banners and blowing up balloons and helping Ginny and Frank set up the equipment he would need. Angel had been so excited about her brother coming home she'd hardly slept a wink the night before; but now she stood, shyly clinging to Frank in the midst of all the welcomes.

"Hey Sissy. Wanna ride?"

That was Eddy Roy; always sensitive to the needs of others. Marianna stifled the instinct to warn them not to hurt his leg. That huge cast wasn't going to let it move, and this was the best therapy she could have thought of, for both her little munchkins. Tomorrow they could worry about treatments and therapy and confronting their son's mysterious insecurity. Today was a day of celebration. Today this family that had suffered too many separations was all together again.

Marianna wakened to find her husband's place beside her empty. She checked her phone. Two o'clock! Had he slept at all? For a moment all the old hurts and fears came rushing back. Immediately, she dived into her waiting Father's arms and sighed with relief as His peace washed over her. She slipped out of bed and padded quietly into the living room. Jaxon stood in his favorite place at the sliding glass door to the patio, silhouetted by the waning moon. He grasped the slender arms she slipped around his waist and drew her close.

She laid her cheek against his broad back and murmured, "Trouble sleeping, Bear? What's wrong?"

He pivoted to kiss the top of her head and lead her onto the fragrant patio. They sat hand in hand, swinging gently in the cushioned glider, drinking in the scents and sounds of the night.

Finally, he broke the silence. "What do you think we should do about Eddy? He's trying his best to pretend nothing's wrong, but his eyes tell a different story."

She wondered if she would ever stop marveling at the amazing changes God was making in their lives. At his worst, Jaxon James Morris II had always been her hero; but at his best, he'd never been very aware of the subtle needs of his wife and kids. Tears of gratitude came to her eyes as she contemplated how often he surprised her now with some unexpected discernment or compassion toward them.

"I wish I knew, Honey. He seems to be constantly wrestling with some sense of inadequacy. It's more noticeable since the accident, but I realize now he's been comparing himself with other kids—especially his big brother—since he was tiny. This just brought it to the surface. Chris and I talked about it this week and he thinks it's a personality thing we're just going to have to help him deal with. Ugh! I was hoping for something simpler, like 'time will take care of it as his leg gets better,' or 'still just getting over the tornado.'" She paused. "I'm grateful you're along for the ride, Jax. To be honest, I'm feeling a little overwhelmed and it helps to know I'm not the only one in this battle."

He turned slightly to regard her sadly before a playful grin crept across his face. "Wel-l-l, I'm glad you're glad I'm losing sleep!" But before she could respond the sorrow was back. "I'm so sorry for all the times I wasn't there for you, Babe. Can't imagine why you stuck it out all those years, but I'm so thankful you did... and so thankful God didn't give up on this stubborn, thickheaded husband of yours."

She leaned into his shoulder and they sat; content to be together, sharing this peaceful, middle-of-the-night reminder of God's patient grace. Then as the first shining rays of dawn slowly defeated the last pale glow of moonlight she murmured thoughtfully, "Pretty amazing, isn't it! He never gave up on either of us, even when we didn't want to know Him. From... from everything I've learned so far, I can't believe God would ever cause bad things to happen to anyone and there's no way I'd want us to re-live the last few years; but have you ever wondered if we'd have ever gotten to know Him—or maybe even gotten to know each other like we do—if it hadn't been for all we've been through? Have you ever thought it might have taken something like this to make us realize Eddy had such a problem?"

He hadn't, he thought, but it was just one more perplexing, fascinating question to take to his weekly study with Frank and Ethan.

　　　　"Is not!"
　　　　"Is too!
　　　　"Is not!
　　　　"Is too!
　　　　"Is not is not! Not not NOT!
　　　　"Is too is too is TO-O-O-O!"

It was the littlest McConnell versus the littlest Morris. They loved each other and played together with amazing harmony, but they were, after all, small children and their butterfly people were...theirs!

"Mommy says my butterfly guy is my very own gardinin." Though the endearing lisp of her first few years was long gone, Emma stumbled slightly over the strange word. Delicate arms stretched out to encompass her world. "He's the biggest, most beautiful angel ever."

"Nuh-uh!" Older and taller by more than a year, EmmaLeah was four-year-old Angelina's hero, but this was just a bridge too far. "*My* angel covered *all of us* up when the tornado came and that's the *biggest*. Besides, Eddy says *our* butterfly guy had the shiniest wings ever." She looked down at chubby little fingers and mumbled, "Wush I'd seen his wings..."

E.J., ever big brother to all of them, stepped in to arbitrate. "I think our butterfly guys don't like it if we fight over 'em. My guy told me it was God that sent them to help us and we aren't ever supposed to pay more attention to them than we do to Him. Besides, I think they'd be sad if you weren't friends anymore, 'specially if it was because of them. Emma, you're biggest. Don't you think you should tell Angel you're sorry?"

The girls looked warily at each other; then down at little bare feet shuffling uncomfortably in the grass. Finally, Emma looked up.

"So-o-r-ry, 'Lina." Only Emma called her that, and at her special name Angelina looked up shyly. "Me, too, Emmy," she whispered hesitantly; then impetuously threw her arms around her friend. "Don't let's be mad anymore."

Ginny had been sitting unnoticed on the patio as the kids' dispute had developed. Bless E.J.'s heart, she thought. She'd just been trying to decide the best way to intervene when he stepped in. However, there was a warning here. The whole country had been intrigued by the "butterfly people of the Joplin Tornado," but if they were actually angels—and she believed they were—they were only messengers and servants. She should probably do a study on all the times in the Bible angels warned not to give them the worship, or even honor, that belongs only to God. In fact, she thought, that would be the perfect subject for their little backyard Bible study the last month before school started. She could begin with Exodus 3:2. What child doesn't love the story of Moses and the burning bush! She rose, excitement building, to find her Bible. "Thanks so much, Father!" she breathed. "Now please give me eyes to see, and most of all, a teachable spirit."

"Da-a-d."

Jaxon jumped as the little voice pierced the darkness. He'd been so engrossed in reviewing the new project; making sure it was ready to launch tomorrow, that he hadn't heard his son open his bedroom door and make his way across the darkened living room to the door. This inviting patio had become his favorite retreat over the months he'd been here with his family; especially on nights he couldn't sleep. Ethan had told him not long ago he still sometimes missed it, even after they'd been in their own home all this time. It had been a priceless night-time haven for his family, too. There was just something so tranquil about it, they'd agreed. Now Jax wondered if it could be because of all the prayers that were embedded here.

"Hey, buddy. Can't sleep? Not hurting, are you?"

The sliding screen squeaked slightly as Eddy moved to join his father. Jax shook his head. The resiliency of children never ceased to amaze him. The mysterious baggage his little guy was carrying didn't seem to keep him from adapting quickly to each new transition, and his skill with the crutches he now used exclusively was impressive. He shifted to hold the glider still as Eddy positioned himself beside him.

"Mom said if I can't sleep I should pray, but I don't think God wants to talk to me. I know you said He's not mad, but..." Jax made himself wait while Eddy struggled with his thoughts. "I-I don't wanna feel this way... Mr. Chris says if I don't talk about it I'll jus' feel worse, but... I don't know..." He floundered to a stop and sat, rigid in the darkness.

"Are you afraid about your leg, son?" Jax didn't know, either, but he had to start somewhere.

"No-o-pe. Not really. Mr. Doc said it's doing great 'n I know he always tells the truth, so..."

Jax stifled a grin. His son Mr. Proper wasn't comfortable calling someone as "important" as Doc by his "first name," but he wanted to please his doctor, so he'd found a way to compromise. "Mr. Doc" seemed to satisfy his sense of decorum, and Jax knew his doctor was enjoying that creative solution as much as his father. He decided to try a different tack.

"You said God doesn't want to talk to you. I can remember feeling that way a few times..." The little head came up in surprise at that. "Usually it's because I don't understand Him very well, yet. But can you tell me why you think so?"

Little hands repeatedly flexed and un-flexed, unconsciously replicating his father's response to frustration. "I don't know. I just pray an' pray an' I just feel worse. Miss Ginny says God always answers when we pray, but... Do you believe that, Dad? Does God always answer your prayers?"

Wow. These middle-of-the-night questions just got harder and harder! Well, honesty was the watchword, he reminded himself, so, "Y'know, son, I don't always feel like it, but from what I'm learning, I think He really does. I think it's just that He doesn't always answer the way we want Him to. Or maybe when we want Him to."

He paused. He wanted to be sure he framed this next question carefully. "Do you feel like telling me what you've been praying about? You don't have to if..."

"I just want you to be proud of me, too." It came in a breathless rush, as if the words clamored to be set free. "I just want you to tell your friends about me like you do J," he finished sadly.

There it was again. How had his youngest son become so convinced he didn't measure up and why were they just recently seeing it? And why were their efforts to reassure him not working? What were they still missing?

He carefully pulled him onto his lap and hugged him close, searching for words. Finally, he whispered into the top of his head, "I'm so sorry you still don't see how much your mom and I love you. And how proud we are that you're our son." Relieved to feel the taut little body slowly relax in his arms, he added, "I think we have a lot more talking to do, but for now..." He didn't have to finish. Eddy Roy was sound asleep.

"I want two. Could I have two pancakes, Dad?"

It was good to see his son's eyes sparkle again. He'd been so excited since his dad had told him he was taking him out for breakfast, just the two of them.

It was Marianna's suggestion. Time alone with his father might help their little bear feel better, she hoped. His father hoped it might be a place where he could begin sorting out what was going on in his youngest son's head. And heart.

"Sky's the limit today, Son," he smiled. "You can have anything you want... as long as it's on the breakfast menu," he hurried to add. This kid would eat ice cream for every meal if you let him.

"Yum! I want blueberry! Two blueberry with blueberry syrup. And one egg. And three bacon. Thanks, Dad!"

Eddy chattered happily as they ate. Almost like the old Eddy Roy, he reflected. But on second thought, he wondered if they'd ever known the real Eddy Roy. This melancholy that was troubling him now was no new thing. It had simply taken a crisis to bring it to the surface. He shook his head and smiled, remembering the discussion at lunch last Friday. It was still a strange concept, but all that had happened the last few years was proving to him that what he'd considered a cliché was actually true: God often uses the worst things in His people's lives to bring about His best for them. Jax could only hope that was what was happening here.

"Doc says you should be able to get your big cast off next week. Bet you're gonna be glad to get that walking cast on so you can get rid of those crutches."

"Yep."

Strange. There was none of the excitement Jax would have expected at that. He tried again.

"He says you probably can be back playing soccer again by the spring season, and your coach told me the other day you could suit out and come to practice this fall, even though you can't play yet. That's pretty exciting, isn't it!"

Uh oh. The curtain fell again as Eddy mumbled into a plate bereft of all but the blueberry syrup still pooling in it, "Not playin' soccer."

Keep it cool, Jax, he warned himself silently. Don't shut him down even more. "Guess that surprises me a little, Ed. I thought you loved soccer, but if you want to play baseball or basketball or something else, that's..."

"Not playin' anything," he interrupted tersely, eyes firmly fixed on anything but his father.

Jax waited, but when Eddy offered no explanation, he risked a gentle, "Why?"

"Not any good," the little boy answered tonelessly.

"Who told you that!" He couldn't keep the indignation out of his voice. If that coach had...

"Just know," came the dejected reply. Then the pain surfaced again. "Mom says Angel draws so good she could prob'ly be an artist an' she's good at dancing an' she's really pretty an' J's good at school an' soccer an' basketball an' everything. An' I can't

59

do anything very good. How come God couldn't make me good at something?"

Tears slipped down sturdy little cheeks—a much too common occurrence now, Jax thought—but before he could respond, Eddy added vehemently, "I don't even care if I get my cast off. Won't make any difference, anyway. Not ever playing anything again, so..." He knuckled the tears away and sat staring into a world that had again become dark and overwhelming.

Jax had thought he was prepared, but this was a complete shock. This child had always been the one who couldn't wait for each new sports season to begin. They'd laughed that he'd never seen a sport he didn't like; when he was barely two years old demanding "thporth" while the other kids watched their kiddy programs. What could possibly have happened?

He was trying to decide what to do next when Eddy hurried on: "Angel's got Mom's first name an' J's got your whole name an' I'm just stupid ole Eddy Roy. Why couldn't you..." He stopped, then, realizing he might have gone too far.

Jaxon was heartsick. This little boy they adored had real problems he was just now beginning to comprehend. They'd always called him the easy kid—the laid-back, go-along-to-get-along one. They'd let it go far too long, but at least now he had a clue where to start.

Eddy watched apprehensively as his father called for their check. "C'mon, Son," he said calmly. "You can bring your juice with you. There's something I want to show you."

"God," he prayed silently, jubilantly, as they drove home, "I don't know if I'll ever get used to how You do things, but right now I couldn't be more thankful. I'm understanding more and more that You do everything for a reason, and it's always at just the right time, whether we know it—or like it—or not."

Only yesterday Jax had come home from work to find his wife sitting in the living room with a cardboard box he'd never seen before, tears falling freely. He re-lived that scene as he drove, so grateful that God was still at work in their lives.

But he hadn't been so sure yesterday when he'd found his wife in tears. "Please, Lord," he'd pled silently, "not another crisis." He just couldn't handle another one.

"Mia, Honey! What's happened?"

He hadn't been able to keep the panic out of his voice, but when she'd looked up he'd been relieved to see a huge smile shining through the tears. Whatever it was, it must be a happy crisis.

"It was just delivered a few minutes ago," she'd said excitedly. "I'd heard there was a group that... I wonder where... how could they have found..." Her laugh had been merrier than he'd heard in months and he'd realized with regret that this thing with Eddy had been taking more toll on her than he'd wanted to see.

After a steadying breath she'd tried again. "Our pictures! Someone found the album miles from here with almost all of them still in it. I don't know how long they were out in the rain and wind, but this group spent months restoring them. Don't ask me how they do that, or how they found us, but I'm so, so grateful. I've just been sitting here going through the memories. I can't begin to tell you how much it means to have part of our family history back. We have to find a way to thank them."

Jax had thought he might shed a few tears himself. He'd never been very sentimental, but this was definitely one of the most caring things anyone could have done for them.

Gratitude overwhelmed him again as they neared home. This could be God's instrument to begin the healing process for his son.

At her husband's quick text, Marianna had set the box on the kitchen divider where the kids gathered for after-school snacks, hurriedly pulling out all the pictures she could find that might help their cause, thankful that the other children were helping Frank clean the pond. Then as their car pulled into the lane, she rushed to gather school pictures and other photos they'd accumulated since the storm, strategically inserting them next to the restored pictures she'd selected.

Eddy looked surprised as his father lifted him carefully onto his stool at the breakfast bar. This was the first time they'd allowed him to risk his favorite perch since the accident. In spite of himself, he was curious—even a little excited. What was going on?

"OK, Son, this is what I wanted to show you. Mom has some pictures…"

Curiosity and excitement immediately turned to disappointment and anger. "It's just a bunch of pictures of me," he whined. "That's not…"

"Look again, Honey." His mother's voice was patient, then stern as she cautioned, "And you might want to adjust your attitude a bit. Now, if you'll try to be a little more respectful, I'll give you a hint."

"So-o-r-r-y," he muttered, unwilling to meet her eyes.

Then to his mother's, "Only some are of you," curiosity overcame childish impatience and he looked up in wonder. "That's not me? Then who…"

"This one right here is my dad," his father said proudly, "Jaxon James Morris—your grandfather—when he was six years old. The one next to him is a picture of me when I was seven. And this one on the other side of you is my dad's dad—your great-grandfather—when he was six. His name was Edward Roy Morris. He was a really, really good baseball player, by the way, and we've always been glad you inherited his athletic abilities."

Eddy sat speechless, eyes round with shock. Finally, he whispered weakly, "Edward Roy… I'm named after… he looks just like… I'm almost…"

His mother stood her big makeup mirror in front of him. "OK, Dad, put your face down here beside your son. Now look at that, Eddy Roy. Haven't you ever noticed how much you look like your father? Why do you think we call you "Little Bear?" Your brother may have Big Bear's name but you, as they say around here, are the 'spittin' image' of him." She took his face in her hands, forcing him to look at her, "And I think it's about time you started acting like him."

"The 'him' that knows Jesus, though," Jax interjected, "not the ugly one that used to live in that ugly house. I know it's been rough since the tornado, Son, but Jesus helped me get over being so mad all the time and He wants to help you, too. Mom and I pray for you every day, but He'll never *make* you behave. You have to decide you want to for yourself and ask Him for help. I'm proud that you look like me, and Gramps and Great-Grampa, but I'll be proudest of all if you start looking like Jesus."

They watched hope, then confusion, then frustration play across the unhappy little face.

"But-but, if I'm like you and Great-Grampa, how come J's so much better…"

"Your brother is two years older than you, Eddy. Of course he's bigger and stronger, just like E.J. is bigger and stronger than he is. But have you ever heard either of them say they don't think you're good at sports? I've heard both of them bragging to the other kids what a good soccer player you are. Seems to me they've been more than happy to show you what they know and help you work on your game. I'm afraid you've been letting envy get in the way of having a good time with your brother and I know it's made him sad sometimes."

"Do you know what 'envy' is, Eddy?" his mother asked.

"Like in the Ten Commandments? Miss Ginny made us memorize them, but I'm not sure what they all mean."

"'Envy' means you aren't happy with what you have and want what someone else has instead. Why do you think it makes God unhappy when we envy someone else?"

"I-I-I don't kn-o-o-o-w," the little boy whined unhappily.

"Eddy," his father probed gently, "do you remember when you made Mom and me those cards for Christmas? How did you feel when we told you how much we loved them?"

Eddy looked at his father, big brown eyes questioning.

"Think how you'd have felt if I'd said I didn't like the one you made me. That I wanted the one you made Mom."

"I'd have been really sad—prob'ly mad. But I... oh-h-h..." Now big brown eyes studied flexing hands briefly; then came up in alarm. "Do you think... I didn't mean... I don't want God to..." He floundered to a stop, staring at his parents as tears gathered in eyes now rapidly changing from sullenness to alarm. "I don't want God to be mad, and I don't wanna be sad anymore! But I don't like... I don't know how..."

Jax resisted the urge to pull his unhappy son into his lap and tell him it would all be OK. How could he ever have thought raising kids was fun—or easy—he wondered uncomfortably. Then he was shocked to hear himself say gently, "Can I tell you what I've found out helps me most when I don't like myself?" At his son's surprised nod he continued, "I'm not very good at it yet, but I'm learning that if I just try to remember Jesus made me, He must want me to be exactly who I am. That means I'd better be thankful and tell Him so. Or even better, try to remember to ask Him to help me be more like Him. Does that make any sense?"

"I gue-e-ss so-o-o," the unhappy little boy nodded tentatively, "but what if I don't *fe-e-el* thankful?

Now Jax wrapped big arms around his son. "Great question, Son, and God knows I still have that problem 'way too much," he laughed sympathetically. "All I can tell you is, when I ask Him to, somehow He takes my 'want to feel thankful' and turns it into a real 'thankful.'"

Suddenly J and Angel exploded into the kitchen.

"Mom, you should see how good the pond... Oh, hey Ed. Did you have fun? What did you get? Dad, I wanna go next time. When do I get my time out with you?"

"Me, too, Daddy, me, too," wheedled the littlest Morris.

At the panicked look on her husband's face, Mom took charge. "Whoa. Wait a minute, kiddos. Special time out with Dad is just that. You only get that when he decides, not because someone else gets to go."

J's eyes fell on the cluttered countertop. "Wow, Ed, I didn't know there were that many pictures of you." Turning a resentful look at his mother, he began, "How come…"

His mother stopped him with a warning look. "Eddy Roy, would you like to tell your big brother what you've just learned about envy?"

"Envy is not likin' what you have and wantin' what someone else has instead," he parroted in a sing-song voice; then turned a triumphant look toward his parents.

"Okay, son," his dad laughed, "looks like our next lesson may need to be about pride, but I'm impressed you remembered the whole thing. Now, J…"

"Not all of 'em is me," Eddy broke in, to his brother's relief. "See if you can tell who's me and who's Da… someone else."

"Seriously?" questioned J. "They all look like…" He peered from his brother to his father, then back at the pictures. "Ok, now I see. I can tell by the haircuts. This is you. This is Dad. This is… who's this? And this?" Suddenly intrigued, he blurted, "Wow, Ed. I always thought it was cool I had Dad's name, but I never noticed you had his looks. Cool! So Dad, is that *your* dad? And that real old yellowy one, is that *his* dad? Wow, so cool. We're a bunch of good lookin' Morris men, aren't we!"

They all laughed uproariously at that, while a grateful mom silently thanked God for the light she saw dawning deep in her younger son's eyes once more.

10

THANKSGIVING IN A WHOLE NEW WAY
November, 2014

Marianna smiled, thinking of her husband's wise counsel about thankfulness to their son. She could still see them sitting right here at this breakfast counter. That turning point in their little boy's life seemed several lifetimes ago now; but today, she thought her heart could not hold one more thankful. She was realistic enough to know this was only a precious interlude in a world that still seemed determined to hurl unexpected sorrow into the best of times, but she was just as determined to be grateful for every moment, good or bad. Right now, their days were exceptionally good.

She looked around the sunny basement kitchen that had been their home the past two years, cluttered with the boxes and crates that held what few possessions they'd accumulated since the storm. At least, she thought wryly, owning so few things made moving a lot easier.

She glanced at the clock on the wall. Two o'clock! No wonder she was hungry. She took her lunch to the patio that had provided such sweet retreat in some of the worst days of their lives. It was an incredibly beautiful November day, amazingly warm for only two weeks before Thanksgiving. It seemed that even the weather was smiling on the new beginning God had given the Morris family. She sighed. She needed to finish that last little bit of packing before Jax got home. Her heart overflowed watching his excitement at finally being able to move their family into their new home. It had been a long four years. She wondered how many other families were still struggling to find their new reality in a world that even now seemed more down than up. It was tempting to feel that they were the only ones still trying to fit all the pieces in place, but as Chris had said, there was enough pain in this community to last a long time.

"I really want to try to do something about that, Lord," she whispered. "We've been so blessed through all this, and You know I want to somehow pass that on. Are You really leading me the way I think You are? You know how my heart hurts to think of all the people that still need help. Is it possible I could actually be a good counselor? Chris seems to think I could be. Now I just need to find the courage to broach the subject with Jax..."

She rose and turned toward the hollow at the back of the yard. "What stories you could tell, little pond," she murmured as she strolled slowly around the cobbled path. "And what a gift you've been to our family. I know the kids will miss you. Guess we'll just have to create our own magic garden."

She'd never been much of a gardener. Never really been interested before, but now she found herself longing to create this same sort of quiet refuge in their new back yard. Thank God for Ginny. She'd enthusiastically agreed to teach her what she needed to know and then immediately scheduled several dates on their calendars to begin planning and shopping. She shook her head. Who could ever have imagined their lives would be so enriched by such a horrible event. Ethan was right; God's ways are so past finding out. She'd probably never really understand why He'd chosen to use that terrifying storm to pour His love into a family that had spent so many generations denying Him, but she was more grateful than she could ever tell Him. Now she just had to find a way to live out that gratitude. Wasn't that what Ethan had said he was doing when Jax had first gotten to know him? It had seemed curious—even dubious—to both of them then. Now she understood.

She turned and hurried back to the house. She needed to get the packing finished so they could take the final loads to the house as soon as the big guy got here. She wasn't sure why, but it suddenly seemed terribly important to be in their new place by Thanksgiving.

She was so looking forward to the holidays. Not at all like last year when she'd thought the best she could do was just make it through and keep looking forward to the day they'd be in their own home again. Undeniably, Thanksgiving and Christmas held a whole new meaning since they'd become Christians, but there was a certain loneliness in knowing their little family was all that was left of the Morris clan. She smiled. She should have known better than to underestimate Ginny and Liz. Somehow, they'd managed to make it a wonderful time of celebration for her family, too. After all, Ginny had declared, this was a family time and they were all family now.

She'd never experienced anything like it. Of course they'd celebrated Thanksgiving Day growing up in Michigan, but it had always been more about food and football than anything else. Last year they'd both found themselves marveling at the gratitude and outpouring of love that had embodied this one, beginning with serving lunch at the Salvation Army Shelter. She'd been so encouraged, hearing about how the McConnell's had stumbled into that tradition when their own lives were still in shambles. Listening to Liz describe her heartache had felt a little like hearing her own story. Granted, she'd never had the kind of spiritual heritage Liz did, but she knew intimately the sorrow of losing everything and feeling isolated from everyone she loved, just as Liz had that first year. And she certainly knew what it was like to dread the holidays.

Liz and Ethan's impulse to turn their sorrow into serving others at a homeless shelter was inspiring—something Marianna could get excited about—and that decision to reach out had, of course, led to their eventual friendship. Still, she'd been concerned about taking the kids into that sort of environment; especially the girls. Some of the men she'd seen standing outside looked pretty scruffy, and she didn't want her little ones exposed to the kind of language she was sure was part of life there.

What they'd experienced instead had been humbling. Angel and Emmy had been at their charming, effervescent best and the obvious joy the two tiny girls stirred in saddened hearts had brought her near tears more than once. And the boys, well, they'd brought a new energy to that poverty-stricken place. They'd chattered for weeks afterward about how much fun it had been to "help other people." God's promises in action, she'd marveled. They'd gone to offer comfort and encouragement to those in need and had come away greatly comforted and encouraged. It really was more blessed to give wasn't it! She couldn't wait to see what God had in store for them this year.

She couldn't have known then that this year would take a disappointing turn.

With Frank and Ginny's help, it hadn't taken long to get that final load moved. Now the four friends sat in the Morris's gleaming new kitchen, sharing a pizza.

"Marianna, I know you'll argue about this," Ginny was saying, "but I don't want you to worry about trying to clean the basement." She held a warning hand up as Marianna started to object. "We leave next week and no one will even be in the house until the first of the year, so there's no hurry.

Besides, Emily Jones needs some extra work, so I'll have her clean when I get back. I'm really sorry I won't have much time to help you get settled here before we leave…" She faltered at the look of shock on her friend's face. "Oh no. You didn't know this is our year to go East," she intoned regretfully. "I thought…" She took a deep breath and tried again. "After Frank was so miraculously healed a few years ago, we realized just how precious every moment is. Since then we've spent every other holiday season with our families in New England. I guess we've all been so busy it's just never come up. I'm so sorry…"

Marianna struggled to keep her voice light. "Well, I can't pretend we won't miss you—last year was such a special time—but I certainly couldn't argue how important it is to spend as much time as you can with family. Seems like we went from trying to juggle competing relatives to being just us in the blink of an eye." It was her turn to flounder then as a thought struck her. "You must have thought I was really selfish to insist on moving out right before you have to leave. We could have stayed… I hate to think of your house sitting empty that long… we could…"

Ginny stopped her with a quick hug. "Thanks, friend, but you need to be in your own home. Stuart and Marg will keep an eye on things." She smiled. "Sure comes in handy having a deputy sheriff as your nearest neighbor. Don't worry, they can see our lane from their house and we'll set the alarm and close the gate. Now, let's get things cleared out enough so you can at least get to your beds. The kids will be bouncing off the walls if they can't sleep in their new rooms tonight."

She couldn't deny she was disappointed. She'd definitely miss these friends who'd been such a stabilizing influence in the midst of their chaos; but they could still serve meals at the Salvation Army with the McConnell's before they had their own celebration, she consoled herself. Maybe she'd even try to have dessert for them here or something. It didn't really matter where they had dinner as long as they kept that wonderful new tradition of serving the homeless.

But she would soon find that God had other traditions in mind.

Liz appeared bright and early the next morning, donuts and coffee in hand. "I wasn't sure you'd be able to find your coffeemaker yet, so-o-o, I was taking no chances," she smiled as Marianna opened the door. "I passed Jax and the boys on the way in. Are you planning to let them finish the semester before you transfer them here?"

"It is going to be a lot of driving but we're going to try. Just hate to make them miss the year-end stuff. It's so important at that age."

By mid-morning the kitchen was nearly done. Marianna had just settled Angel at the breakfast bar with a new set of crayons when Liz's phone rang. She watched her friend's face turn from concern to joy back to concern as she listened.

"OK, Honey," she finally said. "Of course we'll work it out. I'll talk to Dad as soon as he gets home and we'll call you this evening."

"Is Elly OK, Liz? You seem concerned..."

Liz's laugh sounded a little strained. "She'd probably tell you everything is wonderful, but, well... we didn't have a clue... she's always been so transparent... Take a deep breath, Liz," she muttered to herself. "Apparently our daughter has met 'the one' and wants to bring him home for Thanksgiving. At least, home to Northern Missouri. She wants us to meet up at mom and dad's so they can swing by his parents' in Illinois on their way back to school. Life sure can turn on a dime, can't it."

Marianna waited as her friend struggled with her thoughts.

"Oh, who am I kidding!" she suddenly burst out. "I'm so, so sorry to leave you in the middle of all this, my friend, but no way can I wait till tonight to talk to Ethan. Sure hope he doesn't have plans for lunch. I'll call you as soon as I can..." Her husband's phone was ringing as she blew Marianna a quick kiss and rushed out.

She was surprised to find Liz at her door early again the next morning.

"I come bearing bribes," she said a little too brightly as she held out another small bag of donuts. "First I leave you in the lurch; now I have a huge, totally audacious favor to ask. Please, please don't feel you have to say yes. I just can't think of any other way..." She faltered; then rushed on as Marianna poured their coffee, "There's a new family in our block; just moved in from the West Coast last month. They try not to show it but I know they're feeling so alone. They have kids about the kids' ages and I just thought... I hadn't said anything because I knew you and Jax would sympathize—and empathize. I thought you could really give them some encouragement, so I invited them to join us for Thanksgiving. It never occurred to me we wouldn't be home. Now I don't have the heart to withdraw the invitation. I wondered... if I got everything ready before we leave, would you and Jax host them at our house? I'm so sorry. I know you've been looking forward to your first Thanksgiving in your new home and it's bad enough that you're ending up alone again, but I can't think of anything else... I know it would mean so much if..."

"Of course we'll help," Marianna interjected. "We owe you more than we can ever repay and I certainly remember how lonely a new place can feel during the holidays. I'll make you a deal. If you can spend a couple days helping me get the house ready and shopping for what we'll need, we can invite them over here. I have to admit it's pretty intimidating, but it's also kind of exciting to think of using our new place to pass on the blessing you gave us. Now, hand over those donuts. We have a lot to do and almost no time."

Now Liz sat watching the early-morning sun brighten her beautiful new great room. She was so glad she'd let Jax talk her into those floor-to-ceiling windows. He still insisted he was just a glorified plumber, but this past year he'd shown a sense of creativity and innovation neither of them had imagined he had.

She was exhausted, but so grateful! Who would have dreamed when she'd felt such urgency to finish moving that they'd actually entertain here only two weeks later—and complete strangers at that. Those two weeks had been absolute chaos, but somehow it had all come together. And Thanksgiving had been amazing.

Lorrie and Tom Henderson had proven to be delightful guests. They appeared to be the quintessential California family, blond and fit and gregarious, though Marianna thought she sensed a slight wistfulness under those bright smiles.

She would discover as their friendship developed that her instincts had been right. The Henderson's move to Southwest Missouri, like the Morris family's, had been driven by an urgency to leave painful memories and broken dreams behind.

Their sons Brekan and Brian were identical twins, just a few months younger than J. The four boys had connected immediately, and the Morris brothers had enthusiastically given them a tour of their new rooms before they ushered them to the bright, cheerful playroom in the basement, overjoyed to find that their new friends shared their passion for sports and Legos.

The girls were a different matter. Both five-year-olds shyly clung to their mothers until finally Marianna prompted, "Angel, do you think Bella would like to see your Elsa dress?"

"Elsa?" Bella's eyes widened. She turned to Angelina in excitement. "Do it light up? Can I see? When you come to my house you can wear my Anna dress. It sings when you push a little flower and…"

"Leave it to 'Frozen' to break the ice," Lorrie quipped as the girls scampered up the stairs, chattering and giggling. "And to think in only a few years you won't be able to give any of that stuff away."

By the end of the day, the four adults had settled into a comfortable comradery. As Marianna and Jax had shared how their lives had changed in Joplin, Lorrie had nodded in agreement. She and Tom had never felt any particular need for God, either, she'd confided. Not that they had anything against religion—just never had any reason to think about it. Then suddenly they'd found their family wounded, isolated in a new and unfamiliar culture where the people reaching out to them wore a name they'd always looked down upon, and everything she'd believed was seeming somehow more and more shaken. At this point, she admitted, she'd probably be open to just about anything.

Jax had watched Tom's eyes turn from open and friendly to hooded and defensive as his wife had chattered. "Been there, done that, my friend," he'd thought. It was okay, though. He knew the drill by now. It was almost like Someone had already laid out the puzzle pieces and he just had to begin putting them together. He smiled. Sure didn't hurt that Tom's work on the new hospital project was in construction. They already had a common interest. He couldn't wait to talk to Ethan when they got back from Northern Missouri. Maybe it was time for a new member in their Friday lunch Bible study.

11

THE MORE THINGS CHANGE...

Marianna could hardly believe it. It was really happening! As amazing as Thanksgiving and Christmas in their new home had been, she was more than ready to begin this new year. College started next week and she'd be part of a whole new world! A thrill of doubt assailed her. It had been so long. She'd always been a good student, earned her associate's degree at their small community college in Michigan with a 4.0 grade point average, but she was young and single then and so much had changed. Would she be able to do it? How in the world would she be able to keep up with classes and still be the wife and mother she was determined to be? They'd barely gotten settled in their new house and there were still so many things she needed to do to make it the home she wanted... that her family deserved. And that new garden she'd been dreaming of... What had ever possessed her to...

"You'll do fine, Babe."

She jumped at her husband's voice behind her. She'd been so engrossed in her own little world she hadn't heard him come into the room.

"I think you're gonna bless a whole lot of lives when you get your counseling degree, so in the meantime we're all gonna suck it up and make it a team effort. The kids are big enough to start pitching in—you know how excited they are about Mommy going to school—and I talked to Ginny today about the lady that comes in once a week to help her clean." He brushed a strand of hair from her face. "Don't look at me like that. There's no reason you shouldn't have a little help. You've done so much for this family, Mia. It's only right the family does something for you, now." He wrapped big arms around her. "I'm so proud of you, Honey. How I was ever lucky enough to find a woman like you I'll never know, but at least I'm smart enough to do whatever I can to keep her happy. You deserve so much more."

What could she say! Jax might believe she'd do fine, but she was still struggling to believe it. Whatever doubts she still had, though, she'd better figure out how to get rid of right now. There was no way she could let herself fail after this evening.

She'd driven slowly into their new garage, loaded down with books and class materials and huge misgivings, so distracted that for the first time since they'd moved she hadn't thought to whisper her usual "Thank You, Lord." She hadn't even closed the garage door; just absentmindedly left everything in the car and slowly opened the door to the kitchen. There, two very dignified young men—dark hair slicked back, ties just right—stepped forward, courteously offering an arm and escorting her to the elegantly appointed dining room table where her husband—dark hair slicked back, tie just right—waited to seat her in the place of honor. It was the most charming candlelight dinner she'd ever seen. It had been all she could do to hold back tears, especially when Angelina—somewhat bedraggled Bella dress twinkling merrily—solemnly extended a bouquet of bright fall flowers and then hugged her as tight as she could.

It had been a sweet entry into an overwhelming new world. But now she trudged across the windswept campus, shivering so hard it made her back hurt. It was a good thing she'd started out with such determination, she told herself. The past few weeks had been harder than she'd ever imagined. Jax and the kids still bragged on her so much she was determined not to let them down, but right now her self-confidence was about as low as it had ever been. She certainly wasn't the only non-traditional student in her classes, but she still felt like such a fish out of water. She'd always been an A student, but here it was halfway through her first semester and her best efforts still hadn't been enough to raise her GPA above a 2.5. And it hadn't helped yesterday to learn that her lab mate Joel was carrying a strong 4.0, even though he was working full time and helping raise two little boys.

She quickened her pace against the chilling wind. Well, she resolved grimly, if he could do it, she could... somehow...

"Envy is not likin' what you have and wantin' what someone else has instead," a little voice suddenly sang into her memory.

Envy? Where had that thought come from? Insecure, maybe. Frustrated, undoubtedly. Overwhelmed and discouraged, absolutely. But envy? That was... "wantin' what someone else has..." the little voice insisted again.

She didn't know whether to laugh or cry. She might not think she had an envy problem, but apparently God did, and He wasn't going to let her get away it—or with feeling sorry for herself.

"OK, God," she muttered as she slid into her frigid car. "Obviously it's time to get real." Her husband deserved a wife who was honest with him, even if it meant confessing she wasn't doing so well. And her kids could probably learn a lot more from a mom who faced her struggles than one who pretended everything was fine.

Half-frozen fingers fumbled with the key. It's just life in a fallen world, she told herself, but still, going from such excitement and optimism just a few short months ago to this was really disheartening. Finally she let the tears fall, oblivious to everything but her despair, as the car slowly warmed. "This is ridiculous!" she scolded herself. "Compared to the last few years this is nothing. What is wrong with..."

She flinched at the taps on her window.

"Marianna? Are you okay?"

Oh no. Joel, of all people. How embarrassing. But before she could answer he was sliding into the passenger seat beside her.

"Do you need help? Can I call someone for you? Are you sick?"

Well, whoever said God doesn't have a sense of humor, she thought bitterly. It looked like she was going to get real right now, with the very young man who made her feel like such a failure.

Joel listened silently as she poured out her frustration and discouragement. She was just framing a self-conscious apology when he sighed, "Boy, do I remember that feeling! Can't tell you how many times I was ready to drop out last year." He grinned. "Probably would've if it hadn't been for Susan browbeating me into hangin' in. Can't tell you exactly when things fell into place for me, but I'm thinking it was about where you are right now. It's so hard to juggle family and work and school, isn't it. Sometimes even now I'd just like to chuck it all."

Joel? And here she'd thought he had it all together…

"There was a guy in a couple of my classes… kinda took me under his wing… really helped me through some of the rough spots…" He paused hesitantly; then plunged on, "you usually have it so together…" (her head came up at that) "I almost hesitate to even suggest it, but if there's any way I could help… maybe work through some of the problems with you… maybe just be a sympathetic ear if you need it… I know how much it meant for someone to do that for me…"

She couldn't help but smile. It seemed that God not only planned to work on that envy thing with her, but some of that pride thing as well. "You know, my friend, I just may take you up on that," she heard herself saying. "I hate to admit it, but somehow it does help to know someone else has been where I am. Now, where's that hot-rod of yours? The least I can do is give you a lift in my nice warm buggy."

Suddenly she was eager to get home. She had a lot to talk over with her husband.

12

BEAUTY FOR ASHES...

"What's going on, Frank? You sounded pretty grim on the phone. Is Ginny OK?"

"She's fine, Jax. Sorry. Didn't mean to sound like it was the end of the world. We've just got some major decisions to make and I wanted the four of us to brainstorm it. I guess you heard about the 26th Street project falling apart."

That's right! He'd been hearing about it on the news, but he'd been so involved in his own priorities it hadn't occurred to him to worry about one still a year away. Well, that's why Frank and Ethan were running the business. He still had a lot to learn.

Jaxon sat in the pleasant conference room with his mentors and Jerrel Williams, the company's Senior Architect, coffee cup in hand, reviewing the figures they'd just presented. The 26th Street project was a lot more significant to the company, and their livelihoods, than he'd realized. He glanced at the middle-aged black man beside him. What was going on behind that tranquil facade? He hadn't gotten to know Jerrel very well—he'd been Senior Architect at Zimmerman Architectural since its founding and worked out of that office—but he seemed like an okay guy. No surprise, there, he thought. Both Frank and Ethan seemed to have an unerring ability to draw the best in their field.

"So," Ethan was saying, "Frank and I have prayed hard since we realized the city was in trouble with their master plan, and to be honest, now that the library project is on hold, maybe for good, neither of us can see a way to keep all our crews. It kills us both to think of having to let anyone go. So many families are just now able to get on their feet again and we've been so thankful we could hire as many as we have, but…" His voice trailed off and he sat, staring into a suddenly troubling future.

Jaxon's stomach dropped. He couldn't believe he hadn't seen this coming. Of course they'd have to trim back. McConnell Zimmerman's bottom line had been healthy because they'd grown strategically, but the huge 26th Street development was projected as their major source of revenue for the next couple years and they'd passed up some promising possibilities because of it. His heart went out to his friends. How many sleepless nights had led up to this meeting?

He stopped the agonized sigh before it escaped. Well, as the old saying goes, he'd been looking for a job when he'd found this one, so… "Please, Lord," he implored silently, "help me be the kind of encouragement and reassurance these guys have been to me. I know You haven't brought me this far to leave me stranded in the dust. At least, I'm gonna do everything I can to believe that."

"OK, guys." He was relieved to hear that his voice sounded strong and composed. "Since it's my teams that have to go, I obviously need to be the one to tell them. Can you give me a couple days to explore some options before we say anything? I'd like to have something positive to suggest to them." He stared blankly at the table; then mumbled into its polished wood, "And frankly, I'd like to have something going for my family before I drop this on Mia…"

He raised troubled eyes to see the other three staring at him in shock.

"What?" He glanced from one to the other in confusion. "What did I say?"

Ethan was the first to recover. "You think we called you in to fire you? You've got to be kidding, man! We're going to need you more than ever. We'll still want to hang onto as many teams as we can, and they're going to need your leadership. And we're going to need your help building a new strategy."

"We're praying you both will hang in there through this," Frank added. "Ethan and I are reducing our share of the profits—temporarily, we hope—but we're certainly not asking you to do that, and we're trying to get something going so we don't have to ask whatever staff is left after all the adjustments to take a cut. You have the numbers and you know your people. I suggest we spend the weekend praying for the wisdom and discernment we're going to need."

Ethan jumped in again, "I know our tendency will be to protect our wives until we have some answers, but if I've learned anything the past few years it's that I need Liz's partnership and common sense in a crisis. Somehow her prayers seem to have more clout than mine—can't imagine why—so I'm asking Elly to pick up the Littles for the weekend so we can focus on fasting and praying together. Please don't feel pressured, though. God will show you how He wants you to approach Him about this." The silence this time was unifying, each man seeking strength for battles to come. Finally, he drew them back to the present, "Well, unless you have questions or Frank has something else..." he paused; then continued when no one answered, "I'd like to pray for us so we can get out of here and get to work."

They all agreed the weekend had been hard, but possibly one of the best of their lives. Each man had decided to follow Ethan's example, clear his calendar, and spend the time fasting and praying with his wife. Jaxon had never paid much attention to the idea of spiritual fasting, so he and Marianna had spent Friday evening researching and studying what, up till now, had been a totally foreign concept to him. He hadn't been too surprised to discover she'd already been introduced to it in one of her women's Bible studies. He'd been amused, and touched, to watch her try to downplay the fact that she knew so much more than he did. That had been their pattern since they began this Christian journey, hadn't it, he mused. He still had so much to learn about being a spiritual leader for his family. At first the idea of fasting had seemed a little extreme, but maybe this kind of prayer discipline would actually help.

He shook his head in wonder at this God he now served. Who would have guessed last Thanksgiving that simply deciding to follow the Bible's command to entertain strangers would not only bring them new friends, but much needed help at a very difficult time. Lorrie had called. She'd been at Liz's when Elly had gotten home. She knew what it was like to be in a business crisis— remember that's what had brought them to Southwest Missouri. Didn't need to know what this one was, just was pretty sure Marianna and Jax could use some time alone.

"I'm picking the kiddos up in an hour," she'd declared. "We've been promising ours a trip to Kansas to see Big Brutus and this will be the perfect time for it. No arguments, now. Bella and the boys will be thrilled..."

He'd held his breath last night when they'd brought them home—a whole weekend with six kids under ten was a huge challenge—but they'd seemed to truly have had a great time. And even better, the kids still seemed to be friends.

It really was incredible. He'd come to work this morning as excited as he'd ever been about the future, and he sensed the other guys felt the same way. It didn't make sense, but he was learning —again—that he was just beating his head against a wall to try to figure God out. What was it Ethan always said? "God's ways are past finding out?"

What should have been a stressful, crisis-oriented meeting had been, instead, a party. They'd all laughed as Frank had laid out a spread of donuts and fruit and dip and bagels and cream cheese and "all things unhealthy" to celebrate breaking their fast.

"OK, guys," he'd grinned, "obviously you've come up with something you like. Let's hear it."

At Jerrel's nod, Jax had presented the business plan the two of them had developed at the Morris's empty dinner table last night. He'd been pretty uncomfortable making that call to someone he hardly knew—especially a professional with the credentials and background Jerrel had—but it had soon become apparent a relationship between their two families was another unexpected gift God had had waiting just for them.

Marianna had tried her best to be gracious when Jax had suggested they invite them over. She knew how important it was to him to do whatever he could to help save the company. This job had given him such hope for the future, and they both owed its owners more than they could ever repay. But Jerrel and Edith Wilson were so out of their league, so cultured and sophisticated; how could she possibly entertain when she couldn't even offer dinner or snacks? She and Edie had visited briefly at an office event or two and she'd seemed very nice, but how could she hope to keep a woman who'd accomplished so much engaged for a whole evening? The idea of trying to keep from boring her to death—or looking stupid—when it would be pretty much just the two of them, well…

"What is wrong with you, Mia," she'd admonished herself. "It certainly wasn't easy for Jax to risk calling Jerrel. It's the least you can do, and even if you do fall flat on your face, it's only one evening."

She'd been pleasantly surprised, though, and relieved. Her charge for the evening had seemed genuinely glad to be there.

"How kind of you to take your evening for this, Marianna," she'd smiled. "Jerrel tells me you've gone back to school and I can't imagine how busy you must be. I'm not sure I'd have had the courage to take that on with three small children. Now, where are those three little Morris's? I can't wait to meet them."

The children hadn't gotten home until right before the Wilson's arrived. There'd been no time to listen to their excited chatter about Big Brutus, or even to get their baths, so Jax had suggested she call their teen-age neighbor to keep them entertained until bedtime. They all three adored Bailey, but since she was barely more than a kid herself, the harder she'd tried to keep them distracted the more hyperactive they'd become. As Marianna had led the elegantly dressed black woman down the steps to the playroom, she couldn't help but cringe at the bedlam into which they descended.

She needn't have been concerned. By the time she'd finished comforting her embarrassed, apologetic baby-sitter and reassuring her they'd certainly call her again, her dignified guest had calmly gathered three over-stimulated children into a giant beanbag chair and captivated them with slightly embellished tales of a little shepherd boy who grew up to be a great and mighty king. Marianna had watched, enchanted, as each character had come to life with its own unique personality and voice. What was it, she'd thought, that had seemed so familiar? There was something about the way the kids responded to this woman, even shy Angelina, that... Of course! Frank. Drama certainly wasn't his thing, but at heart, this was almost identical to Frank's relationship with children. Ethan called it his pied piper effect. They agreed they'd never seen any child that wasn't immediately drawn to him, and this woman seemed to have the same quality. Strange that the only two people she knew who had such instant rapport with children were childless themselves. But if that was some mysterious plan of God, it was too deep for her...

"I'm sorry, Edie, forgive me. What were you saying?" How embarrassing. She barely knew this impressive woman and she'd already...

But Edie had seemed not to notice. "I think my new friends are getting a little sleepy. May I help them get ready for bed?"

To a chorus of "pleeze Mommy pleezes," their mother had smilingly allowed them to usher their new friend upstairs where she had properly admired their new rooms and then lulled each one to sleep with a soothing song all their own. And by the time both women had kissed each sleeping child good night and tiptoed out, Marianna had been absolutely certain this improbable friendship was no accident.

"OK. Here's the pitch. I have to tell you right up front we couldn't come up with a way to absorb all the lost potential from 26th Street. But we do think it might be possible to keep all our crews and still make a small profit. I'm happy with all my superintendents—wouldn't have kept them if they weren't good— but five of them are really top notch. I'd trust them with anything any time. And Jerrel has five guys who are just as good he can assign to work directly with them as supervising architects. We've come up with six projects we're recommending we bid on. They're scattered across the region; definitely a smaller margin and more risk, but if we convert to construction management we can cut our overhead and possibly even save our clients some money. I'm confident my guys will bring us in on time and budget. The two of us will take the project here in town. It's the biggest—and the shakiest. We'll move Brannigan here to head up the day-to-day as foreman, if he'll agree to the temporary step down, so I'll still be free to oversee all the other projects. I'm hoping all five of the other supers will agree to step down to foreman, too, just until we can build business back up. We're proposing construction staff take a five percent cut, with the understanding that they'll all share up to ten percent of profit. I know you didn't want anyone else to take a cut, but we really think the possibility of coming out even better would soften the impact, and there's something unifying about everyone sharing the bad as well as the good. We discussed the option of switching the teams to independent contractors, but some of them aren't independently bonded and we couldn't in good conscience expect them to take a pay cut and begin paying for that, as well as insurance and workers comp at the same time, so..."

He paused, gazing from one upturned face to the other, gauging reactions; then went on, "Since administrative staff wages are generally lower and they can't actually influence the projects directly, we think they should stay at their current rates. Of course, whether we can make all this work depends on getting those contracts, so we recommend you call a meeting of the entire staff for tomorrow so we can all begin praying together. There have to be questions by now about 26th Street, and the sooner we give them specific information the better. We're pretty sure even the ones who aren't Christians will want to be included, though we'll make it clear they don't have to stay for the prayer part unless they want to."

The meeting had gone even better than they'd hoped. To a man, the crews had chosen to stay with the company, and more than one expressed relief and appreciation that they'd been given the whole picture. At the end of the first week the leadership team came together, grateful that their merciful God was using what could have been a devastating time to draw their people closer together; humbled by their determination to do everything they could to see their company succeed.

Now Marianna lay praying silently for her husband. This was the fifth night he'd tossed and turned almost all night. The past couple days he'd seemed so withdrawn and troubled. Her heart had gone out to him last night when he'd finally confided they had yet to secure even one contract of the six he and Jerrel had identified. Yes, it had been a team decision to go forward, but it was still his bright idea, and he'd been so sure it was the right one. They'd made commitments to the crews and he was just praying he hadn't walked them all into a brick wall. Ethan and Frank were the brothers he'd never had and he owed them so much... She'd longed to say something, do something to help.

Finally she could stand it no longer. She slipped quietly out of bed and padded into the living room where her husband stood at the sliding glass doors, peering bleakly into the night. She slipped her arms around him, laying her cheek on his back in the embrace that usually brought such sweet communion for both of them. But instead of grasping her hands in his normal response, for the first time in years he stiffened; then moved woodenly onto the patio.

But the refuge they'd treasured held no comfort this night. No moon or stars graced patio or pond. The very atmosphere seemed a black and ominous reflection of his spirit. She stood uncertainly for a moment, resolutely telling herself this was not a rejection of her. But try as she might, she could not rein in the old hurts and fears that came rushing back with a vengeance. Finally, breathing a desperate prayer for wisdom and strength, she followed.

"Jax?"

"Go back to bed, Mia. You have class tomorrow and I have some thinking to do."

His voice was cold, husky with anguish and... what?

Her head spun. Old terrors overwhelmed her. Weakened knees anxiously sought a chair at the glass-and-iron patio table. Jaxon James Morris II was suddenly as unreachable as he had ever been before. How could she possibly bear all that turmoil and pain again! How could she face more chaos in their family after they'd tasted such hope.

Stop, Mia! she commanded her panicked spirit. God had not deserted them, even if her husband was struggling right now. She had to believe that...

"I can't, Bear. Not when I know you're out here..." She couldn't restrain the strangled sob that stole into the unfriendly night.

He turned at that, seemingly aware of his wife's pain for the first time, but still he made no move to reach out. He stood, hands rigidly clenched at his sides, as if any move might shatter the fragile control he struggled to command.

"I don't know what to think, Mia," he finally groaned through gritted teeth. Her heart went out to him. He was in such torment. But even now, she realized with relief, there was none of the old anger that had nearly destroyed their family.

"I'm struggling to believe we haven't just accepted a fairytale. I want to trust that God really is, and that He'll always do what's best for our lives. I was so sure of that when we were dealing with Eddy Roy's problems. But now... I can't even think of losing everything we've worked so hard for a second time. I keep playing over and over in my head all the things I've said to the kids and to others—maybe even myself—about His faithfulness, but now all I can see is failure and confusion and I feel so betrayed. If we can't trust where He leads us when things are life or death, what good is faith? Maybe I don't even know what faith is."

The patio where they'd always before found such assurance of God's goodness lay dark and silent. Two figures waited, isolated by disappointment and fear, yearning for the hope and promise of yesterday. Finally, a soft voice bridged the black divide.

"Maybe that's actually what faith is, Honey. Maybe if the way is clear and it all makes sense, you don't need faith. We're both so new at this thing, I sure don't pretend to understand much, but it seems like the times we've had to struggle to trust what we can't see are the times we've grown the most."

Finally the slightest blush of dawn slipped over the horizon and the big figure that had stood like stone slowly seemed to take on flesh. Wordlessly he stumbled to the glider, falling on his knees before it to seek the God he longed to believe. Silently, his wife knelt beside him, slipped her hand in his, and added her prayers to his.

It had somehow been the turning point he'd needed. She'd known it immediately. He'd risen from their altar and with a tired smile and pulled her into a grateful embrace before he headed for the shower. The sun was just peeking through the trees as he backed his big pickup out of the drive, but the light in his eyes as he'd bounded down the steps had told her all she needed to know.

It was another week before the contracts began coming in, but then, one by one, the calls came. All but the big, risky one that would keep the company in the black. Weeks passed, but in spite of several meetings and a final call from Ethan, that nod ultimately went to an out-of-town competitor. It was a blow, but in the end the four who had the most to lose came together before their Lord to attest that His plan was still best, even when they didn't have a clue what He was doing, and they would trust Him with this.

Spring and summer had seemed to fly by. Marianna had managed to finish her first year back in college with a solid 3.4 GPA. Not what she intended to settle for, she vowed, but probably respectable considering... She'd decided to take the summer off. There was really no big hurry to finish except in her own mind, but this time with her family was too precious to miss.

McConnell Zimmerman was humming along. Thanks to the double strength of their crews, all five projects were ahead of schedule and below budget and needed little more than a weekly touch-base from their big leader. In spite of intensive prayer and research, however, no other project significant enough to move them into the black had surfaced.

She'd been so grateful—and relieved—that Jax had cheerfully chosen to pour his unchallenged energy into his family. They picnicked along scenic rivers, spent languid days watching the kids enjoy the city's restored parks, took weekend excursions to historic sites and tourist attractions they'd never known existed in Missouri, and spent evenings with their expanding circle of friends, watching nine little balls of energy play in the yard of the moment. The Henderson's had become an integral part of the group and Tom had, at first somewhat reluctantly, joined the small Bible study the men still enjoyed every Friday. Neither Henderson had yet felt any inclination to turn their lives over to a god they now acknowledged was probably real, but their friends laughingly warned they really didn't stand a chance. There were just too many people praying for them, and the Hound of Heaven was patient, "not willing that any should perish."

Now it was fall, and the kids were happily in their new school. Marianna had found herself looking forward to going back as well, determined that this time she'd reach her goal. Ethan had finally gotten a lead on a project big enough to replace the one they'd lost. The proposal was due in a week and Jax and Jerrel were spending most evenings feverishly working to finish it in time.

More "beauty for ashes," Marianna smiled to herself. Just more excuses to spend time with Edie. Jerrel's wife was about as different from her as you could get, in every way. Tall and stately with black satin skin, Dr. Edith Atkins-Williams had been born into an upper middle class Christian family, carried three earned degrees from Ivy League schools and four more honorary doctorates, enjoyed a brilliant career as a corporate executive, and of course, had never had children. But to Marianna's relief and joy, their first immediate sense of connection had quickly deepened into a profound bond of friendship. Reservations about her lively brood eventually getting on this polished executive's nerves had proven uncalled-for.

"Marianna," Edie had admonished after their mother's third warning to stop being so noisy. "Please let them be themselves. You know I love being with these kids. They're a breath of fresh air in a much too structured life, and I'm grateful God brought us together. Now, tell me about school. Are you over the dreaded 'what-am-I-doing-here' stage yet? As many years as I spent in academia, I never started a new program without struggling with doubts. I hope you'll give me a call if you need some encouragement. I know you're a good student, but I also know you're pretty hard on yourself, so any time you need someone to talk you down off the ledge, remember I'm your girl."

Oh yes, Marianna thought, she certainly would.

The last two weeks had been a real exercise in trusting God's timing, Jax mused. He thoroughly enjoyed this early-morning drive to work, especially during changing seasons, and right now the leaves were in full flaming color. He shook his head. How he could ever have spent most of his life refusing to see that something so spectacular could only be the work of a creative God mystified him now.

He was surprised this morning when Jerrel pulled into the parking lot behind him, and even more surprised that Ethan and Frank were already there. There was no question that Jax was definitely the early morning one of the team. Usually he enjoyed an hour or two of quiet before the others arrived. Maybe they'd finally gotten word on their bid. He just hoped the news was good.

He couldn't read the faces that turned toward him as he entered the conference room. Quickly grabbing a cup of coffee from the credenza, he took his usual place, silently looking a question at first Frank and then Ethan.

"Obviously you haven't heard," Ethan said. Jax thought he could detect a strange mixture of regret and delight. Whatever it was must be pretty big.

"Obviously not. Okay, don't keep us in suspense. What's going on?"

"Well, good news first. I got a call late last night that we got the job! Their timeline is really tight and we're gonna have to kick it into high gear, but with you both on the project I'm sure we have the horses to do it. We'll keep this meeting short, though. I know you'll want to meet with your crew as soon as you can.

Now for the bad news… sad news, actually. We just heard that the job we were so disappointed we didn't get went bust. Big time. And there seems to be some question of possible corruption.

Remains to be seen whether it will take the contractors down with it. We might not have survived if we'd been mixed up in that, and I'm so grateful—and relieved—but..." His voice trailed off thoughtfully and Frank took up the narrative.

"Can't help but be really sad for those companies, though, and all the guys just like us it throws out of work. Let's take a minute to pray for them and then we'd better make hay. Fast."

"Hey Babe. I know you're in class but I just had to let you know before I get busy, we got the job! Don't have to tell you how relieved I am, and how grateful you've put up with my insecurities this past summer. Can't wait to tell you the whole, God-you're-so-amazing story. Have a great day, my Mia. Love ya."

Her heart soared. It was so good to hear the old excitement back in his voice, but she wouldn't have traded this past summer for anything. She'd always consider it a gift from God. "Gifts from You, Father," she amended. "There were just more than I could possibly count. Thank You so much for not giving up on us. I don't think I'll ever understand why, but I'm so grateful You love us like You do."

Jax and Ethan sat in the busy waiting room, nursing cups of stale hospital coffee, waiting for word on their injured employee. Jax's confidence in his foremen had just been confirmed in a most harrowing way. When a cable snapped on the crane setting trusses on Mike's project, without hesitation he'd pushed a young carpenter's apprentice out of harm's way and taken the blow himself.

"Sure wish they'd let us know how he's doing." Ethan muttered. "Any idea what might have caused a cable to break like that, Jax?"

"Not a clue. Cables don't usually just break, and the rental place we've been using has always sent quality equipment up until now. Guess no matter how you try, accidents still happen. Thank

God only the very end of it hit his leg. He should eventually be okay, but he's got a really horrible gash. I have to confess, when I got to the site and found him lying there in all that blood, I was so glad to see that ambulance. But it certainly could have been worse. A broken cable can be deadly, and we're all lucky Mike reacted as quickly as he did. He undoubtedly saved that young apprentice's life, but it's bound to lay him up for a while. They'll let us see him as soon as they get through stitching him up and taking a few more x-rays to be sure nothing's broken."

They sat quietly, watching anxious patients come and go, haunted by another time they'd waited here, longing for news. "Please, God," thought Jax. "Let this outcome be as merciful as that one."

"Gentlemen." The pleasant young nurse beckoned them through the doors and ushered them down the hall. "You can see him now but we want to keep him a few more hours. He lost quite a bit of blood and we're giving him plasma. And we want to be sure he tolerates the antibiotics well before he goes home."

Mike lay on the stark emergency room bed, leg wrapped from thigh to calf, IV dripping slowly. "Sorry, guys," he quipped with forced cheer. "Sure messed up our OSHA rating, didn't I?"

"Yeah," Jax answered huskily. "We were just saying it was really inconsiderate of you to be standing right where that cable was gonna break."

"Jax says you've got a pretty nasty cut, Mike," Ethan said sympathetically. "What are they telling you? Hopefully no lasting damage..."

"Nope. Nothing broken. No permanent muscle damage or anything like that. It's pretty deep and they want me to stay off it a day or so, but I should be able to come back by Monday."

"Only when your doctor says you're ready," cautioned Jax. "The guys said Melanie's out of town. You gonna be able to make it alone the next few days or is she headed back? Do I need to call and reassure her you're okay?"

"Nah-h-h," Mike grunted. "I already called her. She's looked forward to this week with her sister all year and there's no reason for her to cut it short. They gave me these handy-dandy crutches an' some pretty powerful pain meds an' I bet by the time they finally let me out of here I'm gonna be more than ready for several night's sleep. I'd planned to spend the weekend in my recliner anyway—there's several football games on. Mel left me a bunch of meals in the freezer and I can always order a pizza or something so just a ride home will be all I need."

Like so many crises, this one proved to be a mixed blessing. The next few hours of waiting for Mike's dismissal gave the two men time to re-connect in a way they hadn't even realized they'd lost. Ethan would always be his older brother in Christ, Jax mused, and he'd be forever grateful for the impact he'd had on his life. Because Ethan had refused to give up on him, their whole family—and generations to come—had hope for a bright eternity. He'd just opened his mouth to tell him how much he appreciated that when his phone buzzed.

"Hey, Boss" came the jaunty, somewhat slurred voice. "I am so ready to go home." By the time they'd wheeled Mike to the car and driven the mile or so to his house, he was obviously feeling the effects of those powerful pain meds. Jax was tempted to record him on his phone, just for laughs when Melanie got home. A man as rugged as Mike giggling like a school girl was definitely worth preserving. On second thought, though...

It actually turned out to be two weeks before Mike was released for work. The wound had been so deep and there had been so much bruising, the doctor explained, that they wanted to be sure the tissue below had healed enough to bear his weight.

On day six Jax had looked up to see him leaning on his crutches, silently watching his crew work. Words of warning had died in his throat as he'd suddenly remembered another rough and rugged man, leaning forlornly on a cane, longing for the day he could work again. Nobody understood where Mike was right now better than he did, and he hadn't even been by to see him since Melanie had gotten home. Well, he'd fix that tonight, he'd thought remorsefully. He'd called Marianna right then. Of course she wanted to go with him, she'd answered, and she just had time to fix them one of her famous casseroles.

He'd stepped back where he could watch without being seen as first one, then another of Mike's team found a reason to wander over to where he stood, gently knuckling him on the shoulder, admiring the bandage that still swallowed his leg, joking loudly that, "Some people would do anything to get out of work." The young apprentice Mike had pushed to safety was the last to approach. Eyes downcast, he stammered, "Mike, I didn't know how... How can I ever... That cable could have cut me in two..."

Mike good-naturedly dismissed him with a swipe of his crutch. "Ahh. Don't make a big deal of it, kid. It was just reflex action. You'd have done the same thing. Besides, I didn't want to have to fill out all that worker's comp paperwork. Now, get back to work. You're needed." Then as the young man turned, he called out, "Hey, you're a good man, Charlie Brown. Glad you weren't hurt."

Big, crude Arlo jumped in with a grin, "Yeah, Charlie, but don't feel too important. Mikey just did it for us. The world couldn't stand two Charlie Brown's."

Thanks, Arlo, Jax smiled silently, as the men laughed raucously, slapping Charlie on the back. You just broke the ice for everyone, especially a very young man called Charlie Brown.

13

WEEPING MAY ENDURE FOR THE NIGHT...

It just couldn't be possible! They'd just had dinner together two nights ago. How could their beautiful, dynamic friend be gone! No one, not even Jerrel, had any inkling of a single weakness in Edie Wilson's strong, graceful body. She'd simply gone to bed, told her adoring husband she loved him more, turned over and slept, and quietly gone to be with Lord she loved even more!

Jerrel, of course, was devastated, but they were already seeing the calm spirit of trust that they'd come to expect in him, even in this. Jax and Marianna had immediately gotten a sitter and driven to the Williams home in Carthage to be with him. They would spend the next few days there, helping field the calls and visitors that never seemed to stop. They watched in awe as this quiet man met them all right where they were, often being the one to console and encourage them in their loss. And what a tribute to his wife it had been. Students from the evening classes she taught at the university overflowed his living room, sharing story after story of kindnesses and stern admonitions that had changed their lives. Generations of "Edie's kids" from her Sunday morning Bible class joined the litany of appreciation. Young women she'd mentored over the years came to speak of the wisdom and love she'd poured into their lives. Laughter and tears embroidered hugs and shared memories and they stayed to comfort each other as grieving family.

Marianna thought her heart just might break. In the short year she'd known her friend she'd come to love and admire her as the mother to whom she'd never been able to feel close. Edie had always been there with a hug or challenge or listening ear. Marianna thought she might have learned more from her than anyone she'd ever known, even Liz and Ginny, who were, of course, at the top of her list of most admired.

Then they were all gone, back to lives that still seemed normal. Marianna had sent Jax home to put the kids to bed while she stayed to help Jerrel store the latest round of casseroles and cakes and crockpot dinners. The house seemed so quiet she worried how he would deal with it when she was gone. And suddenly her own loss hit with such force it took her breath away. Up until now she'd been so focused on Jerrel and their family there's been no time to confront her own grief. Now it would not be denied. Suddenly the reality of it all struck home. No Edie to call when the assignment didn't make sense or the instructor seemed totally unreasonable. No mother-friend to pin her with big, dark eyes when she was being unreasonable in her own right. No warm embrace to reassure her that God loved her no matter what. How could she ever make the kids understand why their beloved Miss Edie would never again be there to tell them stories about kings and shepherds and talking donkeys? If only she'd taken the time to video those wonderful moments. If only she'd remembered how fleeting such moments are.

Why couldn't God have let them have her just a little longer? Surely He could have intervened to save her... awakened Jerrel in time... made sure the attack happened during the day when someone would see. Why...

"Jerrel," she whispered tentatively, "do you ever ask God 'why?'"

Big brown eyes so reminiscent of his wife's pinned her with that same parental look. "Do you want to ask Him 'why,' Marianna?"

Suddenly the dam broke. She wanted to be strong for her friend, but the sobs just would not stop. "She was more my mom than my mom ever was, Jerrel! I don't understand why God would take her away when we all need her so much. It's so unfair! Why would He leave you here alone when you've both served Him so well? It scares me that I don't want to just ask Him, I want to shake my fist and holler at Him. After all He's done for my family, I'm still so angry..."

He didn't say a word, just held out big brown arms to hold her until the sobs were spent. Finally, he took her by the shoulders to peer into her eyes. "He's a pretty big God, my dear. I'm sure He can handle our whys, and He'd much rather we talk to Him about it than try to handle it on our own. And yes, I confess, in the middle of the night I've shouted a few whys at Him myself. Sometimes I'm not sure how I'm going to make it through the rest of my life without her. But then I think of her strength when her sister died right after her father was killed in that horrible accident; or I remember how she chose to trust His plan when we got the news we'd never have children, and I hear her remind me of the hope He always has waiting for us and I want her to be proud of me." In spite of his resolve, a strangled sob escaped. He gazed thoughtfully at the wall above her head a moment and then finished decisively, "Most of all, I want my Jesus to be proud of me. Now, young lady, you need to get home to that family of yours. Thank you for staying. You know we love you and Jax, and I'm so grateful for the joy you and the kids brought my Edie in her last year here. Please always find comfort in that."

14

...BUT JOY...

They all agreed. This was exactly what Jerrel needed. They were more than grateful for the refuge and diversion the new project afforded their bereaved friend. The first few weeks were a whirlwind of procuring bids and assembling teams and finalizing timelines and estimates, and by the time they left late each evening they were all exhausted. They watched closely as he came in each day, to all appearances hopeful for the future and ready for whatever the day held, though there was an indefinable sadness that always seemed to lie just below the surface. Time, thought Ethan. Only time would dull the pain that seemed to strike out of nowhere at the most unexpected moments. Well, he mused, it was a price one paid for the depth of relationship one built in Jesus. A price he knew they were all more than willing to pay.

By late October walls were going up on the huge new church development project. Jax came home each evening humbled at the hard work and dedication he saw in his men. What a testament to the power a lot of prayer and a little ownership could bring, he exulted. He'd never seen a job where every single man seemed determined to outwork the others, but he was loving it.

Now it was Friday and they were dragging. It had been such a heavy week. He knew they were all looking forward as much as he was to some rest this weekend, and he couldn't help but be a little perplexed that Ethan would call a meeting so late in the week. Of everyone. That would put them all on pins and needles, he thought, but he knew his friends. They didn't do anything frivolously, so he made the calls and headed for the McConnell Building.

What in the... This was definitely a surprise! Balloons and streamers festooned the entry, and as the men entered they were escorted with great fanfare, along with their waiting families, to the conference room. There a huge buffet waited under more streamers and balloons. What a zoo, he thought, and what a wonderful way to say thanks!

"Today," Frank boomed as they crowded into the usually-spacious area, "we break even! Two months ahead of schedule. You all are amazing and we just had to celebrate. Don't even look at it as a bribe to keep up the good work," he added to scattered chuckles and comments. "Some of your wives were disappointed not to have to cook tonight," more chuckles and oh yeah's, "but we thought it was the least we could do. We really do believe we have the best of the best and we aims to keep ya happy, so, Jax is gonna pray and then let's dig in."

Marianna shot a concerned glance at her husband. To her knowledge he'd never had to pray publicly without warning before. She needn't have worried. He calmly bowed his head, grabbed her hand, took a deep breath, and talked to his Father about how grateful they all were for His blessings.

"OK, kids first," Ginny decreed. "As soon as you're finished eating and your parents excuse you, we have games set up in the back... including...tum-ta-dum-dum... a bounce house! But nobody outside until we're all finished eating. Miss Liz and I will meet you there in forty-five minutes."

How in the world had they pulled this off, Jax wondered, without anyone knowing. He thought he'd never known anyone who found more joy in bringing happiness to others than these people. And they called him "friend." Amazing. And humbling.

15

HOPE AND A FUTURE

"How's it coming, Bear?"

Marianna set a tall glass of iced tea on the desk by his hand and slipped her arms around him, leaning to rest her cheek on his head. He'd been hunched over that desk all morning.

Jax sighed and leaned back into her embrace.

"Why in the world I ever let myself be talked into this... I am so out of my element."

"OK, here's where I use your own words against you. And I quote," she teased lightly, "'If it's what God's called you to do, He'll make sure you can do it.' We both have great confidence in you, Jaxon James Morris. You've done some pretty awesome things this past five years, and I think He's just getting started with you."

"Yeah, well, He's got His hands full with this one. Are you getting lots of studying done? It was good of Liz to take the kids, but the house is almost too quiet."

"I know. I keep thinking I need to go see what they're doing. And to answer your question, studying's going about like your speech is. Still have a week before finals, though, and I'll get there. I'm excited about graduating, but I have to admit I'd be more excited if I could forget that I'm only getting started. Two more years like the last two before I get my master's sounds like an awful lot more school right now. Maybe we both need a break. Let's go see what else is blooming today."

Marianna had fallen in love with her garden. It had become her greatest pleasure—her refuge when her busy soul needed soothing. It seemed like God always had some little life lesson waiting there. Maybe someday she'd write a book about "God's Little Lessons from the Garden." Maybe she should start keeping notes...

They strolled hand in hand along the cobbled path Ginny had helped her install. Stones and liner for the little pond that was still her dream lay waiting. It was next on her list, just as soon as graduation and all the celebrations were over.

She could hardly believe it had been five years. At times it seemed like only yesterday that monster storm had devastated their town and changed their lives so drastically. At other times it felt like five lifetimes had passed. Who could have ever dreamed, in those first few terrible months, that the end result could be this! Or that they would fall in love with the God they'd so carelessly denied their whole lives.

"I guess I'll never be able to say it enough, Father," she thought. "I can't possibly understand why You bothered with such stubborn children, but I'm so grateful You did... and do."

She glanced at her husband.

"Yep," he smiled.

"Yep," she agreed.

Joplin had been gearing up for its big five-year anniversary all year. In some ways, the area had become a textbook study of what the experts all said to expect after a major disaster. Leadership that had led them through the worst of times had fallen out of favor and moved on to other, less fractious communities. Citizens who'd been so united in tragedy found themselves at odds in triumph. Plans that had looked so bright and hopeful had proven impossible, or at best, disappointing. Churches that had led the recovery were struggling.

But underneath it all, Jax knew that vaunted "something different about Joplin" still remained. At its core the city was still a place that honored God and cared for its people and reached out to others in distress. He needed to be sure he included that in his speech somehow, he thought. That, and how miraculously those values had changed and healed his family.

It was such an encouragement to drive down South Range Line these days. It was becoming almost impossible to remember how completely ruined that whole area had been just five years ago. Now it was thriving. New businesses were still opening almost every week. And his job was helping put those buildings back in place, he thought gratefully. Who would have ever believed it. Could it be only three years ago that he'd stood in the door of that dreary little trailer, miserable and terrified, cursing everything that had brought him there?

He still couldn't help but feel a little depressed at times, though, at the contrast between South Range Line and South Main Street just a couple miles to the west. From the city's old business district along that street to the former St. John's Hospital site farther west, restoration still lagged behind all the rest; still held too many reminders of that horrific time. Too many empty concrete slabs and roughly-bulldozed lots still interposed themselves among gleaming new businesses and renovated homes.

Finally, however, that region too was slowly being rebuilt. A tranquil new memorial park now stood on the site of the most unthinkable loss of all. A butterfly garden was said to be in the works to celebrate the mysterious "butterfly people" that were so much a part of the Joplin story. New, state-of-the-art schools and parks inhabited all parts of town; including a new water park at historic Schifferdecker Park in the northwest. The impressive new Mercy Hospital complex was up and running southeast of the city, and the ambitious public library venture on West 26th Street was finally on track to begin soon. Frank and Ethan were truly happy to hear the problems had been resolved, but they'd decided not to re-bid the job. Their high-profile church project had given them all the exposure and credibility they needed and right now they were attracting more business than they wanted to try to handle.

Jax shook his head, smiling ruefully. Only the mysterious God he now believed in would tap someone like him on the shoulder to try to tell that amazing story to their world. What was it their pastor had said last week? "Often He chooses the weak to confound the strong." There'd been a time, he thought, that the idea of being weak in any way would have set his teeth on edge. Now, he was finding it a curious comfort. Now he knew all the strength he ever thought he had—even if he could have combined it with Pops'—was nothing compared to the Creator of Heaven and Earth. And incredibly, that Creator was his Heavenly Father! And somehow, mysteriously, that was all the strength he'd ever need. Well, okay then.

May 22, 2016

Today was the big day. Like that fateful Sunday in 2011, towns across the region were celebrating graduations; and the friends had met after church to cheer Marianna across the stage to receive her diploma. Today their favorite South Range Line restaurant was again the site of happy celebration. Still, thought Liz, though the cast of characters had changed a bit, it was all too eerily reminiscent of that terrifying time. The weather had been amazingly mild all winter; spring had blossomed at least a month before it was due and this day was as fresh and sunny and perfect as that Sunday five years ago. How many others would find themselves watching the skies for signs of gathering storms, she wondered. And no matter how much she admonished herself to be logical, she couldn't help but hold her breath at the thought of what might be waiting at that pleasant restaurant's entrance. She would not have been at all surprised to see the bushes there once again filled with giant butterflies.

It was so good to have everyone all together again. The trip to Illinois for Elly and Brennan's college graduation had been exuberantly hectic, but it was good to be home. She darted a glance at her parents, sitting next to the Morris's. Not surprisingly, Big Mike and big Jaxon had discovered an immediate rapport; shared values of hard work and devotion to family transcending the generations between them. Or maybe, she reflected, Jax had found a little of the father he still missed in her own father. They were all tired, but it was a good tired. Especially after their daughter and her fiancé had arrived this morning in time for church, and almost at the same moment, to everyone's joyful surprise, Alison and her new husband had appeared. All four young people were planning to be here for the full week of celebration and now Liz sat watching them laugh and chat. Ali had recovered almost complete use of her shattered arm and the residual scars could only be seen if one looked very closely. Both her girls had chosen well, she thought with satisfaction, and their guys seemed to have formed a bond of friendship that would help keep their families close through the years. What a blessing that friendship would be, she thought gratefully, like their friendship with Frank and Ginny. What would their family have done without them the last few years!

It would be good to have their daughter home one last summer while they planned her wedding. The date was set for early fall. It seemed completely right that the ceremony would be at the little garden pond where Elly had fought and won her greatest battle of faith, and Ginny was ecstatic to think of pampering her favorite child on her most important day. (They all smiled at that. Every child was Ginny's favorite child.)

The Little's had never stopped missing their big sister, even though for the last four years they'd only seen her on holidays and summer breaks; but now they seemed almost as excited to see Brennan as they were Elly. From the beginning, that young man had seemed to understand their need for attention from his future wife, and he made sure any time they were in Joplin, outings with her siblings were first on the agenda. He'd won his future mother-in-law's heart forever when she'd realized he was quietly inviting them along on many of their dates, and now she watched appreciatively as he nonchalantly moved around the table to make room for both children between himself and his fiancée. What a wonderful father her daughter had chosen for their grandchildren, she thought jubilantly.

Jax had been touched that this year his family had been included in their celebration—you're family, too, they'd reminded them—but a bad case of nerves had made it impossible for him to eat a thing, in spite of the tantalizing sights and aromas. It had helped, though, to just sit back and soak up the love and care for each other he'd seen around the table.

He thought back to the cloudy Saturday a month or so ago that had brought him to this point. He hadn't recognized the big black sedan as it pulled slowly to the curb in front of their house. He'd watched closely as a passenger had rolled down a window and spoken briefly to the children. Normally they didn't allow them to play on the front walk, but they'd been excited about trying out their new scooters and he and their mom would be right there, so he'd said yes. Just this one time, though. This was about as safe a neighborhood as you could find, but still...

He and Marianna had spent the morning trimming shrubs and cleaning out the last of the winter mulch from around the roses that fronted their brick-and-stone home. He knew she was a little embarrassed to face the nicely-dressed man and woman who approached their walk, so he'd greeted them there while she slipped quietly inside.

"Seriously? I'm sorry. I don't mean to be rude, but... why in the world would you want me to speak at the Anniversary Ceremony? Are you sure you have the right person?" He'd wanted to add, "I'm a plumber, not a speaker," but he'd restrained himself. Only his friends would understand that little bit of humor.

They'd smilingly assured him, however, that yes, if he was Jaxon J. Morris, who'd lived in FEMA Village several years, he definitely was the right person. They'd been looking for tornado survivors with stories of butterfly people and unexplained miracles and successful recovery to tell, and, well, he'd probably be surprised how many people had given them his name. What made them even more excited about hearing from him, they'd added, was that time in FEMA Village. Absolutely, they wanted it all; from the leg that refused to heal to the kindness of friends who took them in to his eventual success in creating a new career for himself. Surely survivors of any disaster could be encouraged by that story. Of course they understood, and heartily approved that he'd only tell it if he could give God the credit. How could anyone understand the story of Joplin, MO, without including—and honoring—the One Who'd made their city a watchword among all who struggled with such things? And yes, they'd respect his need for time to think and pray about their request. Please let them know as soon as he could though. They were praying he'd say yes. There were so many who still needed to hear from overcomers like him.

"But *you're* the real overcomer, Babe," he'd argued when Marianna had excitedly urged him to accept. "You're the one they should be hearing from. Without your patience and faith, we might not even be a family by now. I'd feel like a fraud, standing up there, when everyone who knows us understands exactly who the strong one really is. Besides, you're definitely a much better speaker."

As usual, his wife's logic had prevailed. Finally he had to agree, he was the one God had kept tapping on the shoulder, in spite of his stubborn resistance, and yep, he certainly could tell that story.

Now he stood, peering out uneasily from his designated post backstage. He stretched tense shoulder muscles and wondered for the thousandth time how in the world he'd let himself be talked into this. Though he certainly appreciated how important this day was to the city's healing, he'd be so glad when it was over. He'd never pretended to be a speaker—never even thought he'd want to be. What could he possibly share that someone else couldn't do so much better! But his friends, and of course his wife, had all insisted that this was what God expected. And he had agreed, of course, that the world should know how much He cares for each one of them; and most certainly must be honored for all that He'd done for his family. So here he was, waiting for his cue to go on stage before that huge crowd.

"Please, God," he prayed silently, "what You've done in our lives is so amazing. Please help me tell our story in a way that leaves people touched by who *You* are."

He felt a gentle hand slip into his and glanced over to see his wife praying at his side. She'd be right here while he spoke, she'd promised, praying; and yes, she'd be glad to bring the kids out to be introduced when he was finished. As usual, she'd straightened him out when he'd argued that they all should be on stage while he spoke, rationalizing that it was their story, too. "Actually, it's God's story," she'd reminded him with a smile. Well, she was right about that, and now he just wanted to tell the story that would bring this awesome God Who'd shown them such undeserved mercy the honor that was rightfully His.

It was time! He drew a deep, steadying breath as the MC announced loudly, "Please welcome Jaxon Morris!" No backing out now. He squared his shoulders and strode to the podium. Wow. This crowd was enormous. He stood, silently gazing at these people who had become his friends and neighbors as the crowd hushed expectantly.

"Hi," he said, pleasantly surprised at the calm strength of his voice. "I'm Jaxon James Morris, II, from Detroit, Michigan. I'm here tonight to tell you how God brought our family to Southwest Missouri right before the Storm of the Century so He could use a bunch of ugly standpipes and storm shelters to give us His hope and a future...

EPILOGUE

Though characters in this book are strictly fictitious, the story of Joplin, MO and its long recovery from the 2011 EF5 tornado is real. Jaxon Morris and his family represent those last few FEMA Village residents who struggled to find a new reality and rebuild devastated lives long after most people had gone back to normal, everyday living.

Today, much like Ali's shattered arm, scars along the city's shattered thoroughfares can still be seen, but only if one looks closely. Some scars that remain on the city's wounded spirit are easier to see. Civic government struggles to restore lost trust and regain credibility. Bureaucracies struggle to honor the past and keep moving forward. And suddenly, without warning, some families struggle to recover from the "Hundred Year Flood" that engulfed their homes the last week of 2015.

Our daughter Kim's house south of Joplin, where we huddled with two frightened young women as the tornado roared overhead, is one of those. Our granddaughter Carissa's house, where she and her children settled after they lost everything to the tornado, is another. One always thinks that, at least with a flood there should be enough warning to save precious possessions. We've discovered that often there is not. The night after Christmas, Kim, her son Kyle, and his wife Emily found themselves literally running for their lives across pitch black fields, struggling to help elderly neighbors also fleeing the flood, as the water rose several feet in only minutes.

FEMA is once again a presence in this region. No FEMA Village for this disaster, though. Only scattered families, working to pick up the pieces and start over again, some for the second time in five years.

Kim is starting over alone. Our larger-than-life son-in-law, who so miraculously survived the tornado in that exposed SUV, did not survive the massive stroke that felled him without warning only three years later. If there were any whys in the middle of his courageous wife's night, though, they never saw the light of day. Instead, according to her, it is what it is. One simply faces one's fears, testifies that God is faithful, and does the next thing.

But while the disaster is smaller in scale and the FEMA experience is not the same, the outpouring of love and service among God's people is. As soon as word went out and the water went down, Kim's house was inundated once again; this time with friends and family and church armed with shovels and masks and rubber gloves, ready to take on the grueling job of demolition and salvage one more time. Others would come to help rebuild and restore. And still others are waiting to finish outside repair and clean salvaged contents and help with the exciting move back home.

As Joplin observes the five-year anniversary of its worst disaster in more than a century, it is true many lives will never be the same. But this one thing is clear: In spite of it all, the heart of Joplin remains strong. There is still something different about Joplin. God is still here.

ABOUT THE AUTHOR

Sandi McReynolds is a life-long resident of Southwest Missouri. She lives with her husband, Mac, and "the Boys," two Shih Tzu/Jack Russell Terriers, and a giant rescue mutt called Ditch Dog, just outside of Joplin. Like most members of the region, she and her family were profoundly affected by the monstrous Joplin tornado of 2011. *Butterflies at the Window,* her previous novel about the storm, was based on their true experiences and the mysterious "butterfly people" children of the tornado were insisting they saw. *Standpipes and Storm Shelters* is "the rest of the story;" a tribute to all who refuse to be defeated by the storms of life and most of all, to a loving God Whose plans are always good,

www.ingramcontent.com/pod-product-compliance
Lightning Source LLC
Chambersburg PA
CBHW070629130626
46555CB00006B/2487